Grade

1

Learn to Read

With Classic Stories

McGraw Hill Children's Publishing

Columbus, Ohio

Acknowledgments

McGraw-Hill Children's Publishing Editorial/Art & Design Team

Vincent F. Douglas, *President*
Tracey E. Dils, *Publisher*
Phyllis Armelie Sibbing, B.S. Ed., *Project Editor*
Andrea Pelleschi, *Story Editor*
Rose Audette, *Art Director*
Jennifer Bowers, *Interior Layout Design and Production*

Also Thanks to:

Andrea Pelleschi, Claire Daniel, and Melissa Blackwell Burke, *Story Retellers*
Edith Reynolds, M.S. Ed., *Editor*
Nancy Holt Johnson, B.S. Ed., *Editor*
    Story Illustrations:
        Reggie Holladay, *The Little Red Hen*
        David Christensen, *The Magic Fish*
        Guy Porfirio, *Jack and the Beanstalk*
        Loretta Lustig, *The Ugly Duckling*
        Kathleen McCord, *Aesop's Fables*
        CD Hullinger, *Johnny Appleseed*
    Activity Illustrations:
        Reggie Holladay, *The Little Red Hen*
        David Christensen, *The Magic Fish*
        Carlotta Tormey, *Jack and the Beanstalk*
        Linda Howard Bittner, *The Ugly Duckling*
        Linda Howard Bittner, *Aesop's Fables*
        Burgandy Beam, *Johnny Appleseed*

McGraw Hill Children's Publishing

Published by American Education Publishing, an imprint of McGraw-Hill Children's Publishing.
Copyright © 2004 McGraw-Hill Children's Publishing.

Send all inquires to:
McGraw-Hill Children's Publishing
8720 Orion Place
Columbus, OH 43240-2111

ISBN 0-7696-3351-X

1 2 3 4 5 6 7 8 9 WAL 09 08 07 06 05 04

Table of Contents

Introduction for Parents and Teachers

The Importance of Reading Classic Tales

Storytelling is an art that started long before stories were recorded and published. Orally passed from storyteller to storyteller in front of a crackling fire, many stories changed form, yet maintained similar plots and themes. We may credit these tales to names such as Jacob and Wilhelm Grimm, Charles Perrault, Joseph Jacobs, and Jørgensen and Moe, but in fact, these storytellers collected century-old stories from oral sources, crafted them, and wrote them down in the form we now enjoy.

Classic fairy tales and folk tales around the world are similar in their themes of good versus evil and intelligence or cleverness versus force or might. The details of the stories may change, but the themes remain universal.

Many fairy tales contain elements or suggestions of violence, such as the threat of being eaten by giants, witches, or ferocious wolves. In part, this violent bent emerged because early fairy tales were intended primarily for an adult audience, not for children. Fairies were often cast as the rich and powerful, with the main human character representing the poor, oppressed common person. The tales served as beacons of hope for the underprivileged in ancient times when there was little chance for social mobility.

Many psychologists today believe that fairy tales are good for children, because these tales represent what all people fear and desire, and thus help children face their own fears and wishes. Other psychologists say that children benefit from hearing stories with some element of danger, and then being reassured with happy endings in which the small, apparently powerless hero or heroine triumphs after all. This is especially true when a supportive parent takes the time to discuss the stories with his or her child and provide specific, personal reassurance.

Knowing classic stories and their characters will help ensure that your child begins to have a rich background in cultural literacy. Classic stories also expand the world of children by enriching their lives and empowering their learning. The tales present characters who undergo struggles and emerge transformed, thereby helping readers discover more about themselves. When your child identifies with these characters, he or she might better understand his or her own feelings and the feelings of other people.

Classic stories present diverse cultures, new ideas, and clever problem-solving. They use language in creative and colorful ways and serve as a springboard for your child's writing. Most of all, classic stories delight and entertain readers of all ages by providing the youngest reader with a solid base for a lifelong love of literature and reading.

About This Book

Learn to Read With Classic Stories has two main parts—the classic stories and the reading activities. The **classic stories** are a collection of fairy tales, folk tales, and fables. This collection may be read and reread regularly. Kindergartners and first graders will probably need some help reading the stories. Second and third graders should be able to read the stories more independently. When the book is finished, it can be saved as an anthology to begin or add to your child's home library.

Follow-up **reading activities** are included for each story to build your child's vocabulary and comprehension skills. These activities focus on skills such as phonics, word meaning, sequencing, main idea, cause and effect, and comparing and contrasting. Additional language arts activities center on grammar, punctuation, and writing. A unique feature to this book is that the activities are closely linked to the stories and not presented in isolation. They are taught within the context of the story. The benefit of this feature is a more meaningful learning experience.

Kindergartners and first graders will probably need help reading the directions, but children of this age should be able to complete the activities with a minimum of assistance. Second and third graders should be able to complete the activities more independently.

The activity pages are perforated for easy removal. There is also an **answer key** at the end of the book for immediate feedback.

A one-page **bibliography** at the end of each story is provided to guide you and your child to further reading. This list contains other tellings of the same story, usually one traditional and one with a twist, so your child can compare different approaches to the same story. Several enjoyable, age-appropriate books that are related in other ways to the story are provided as well. This list of books will come in handy during visits to the library.

A **reading skills checklist** on pages 295–296 can help you monitor your child's progress in reading comprehension. Of course, no two children progress at the same rate, but the checklist suggests appropriate reading goals for your child. Sample questions are listed for each skill. You may ask these before, during, or after reading to assess your child's ability to apply the skills.

At the end of the book you will find several pages of **everyday learning activities** you can do with your child in the subject areas of reading, writing, science, social studies, and arts and crafts. These activities will extend your child's learning beyond this book.

About "The Little Red Hen"

"The Little Red Hen" is an English folk tale, and it was likely passed from storyteller to storyteller for many years before it was written down. The first person known to have written and published the story was Joseph Jacobs, well-known in the late nineteenth century for his popular retellings of and scholarly writings about English folklore. Since then, many writers and artists have recorded many different versions of the story.

In all versions of this folk tale, the little red hen is the hard-working main character. Usually, there is a cat who is lazy and does not want to help. Depending on the storyteller, the other characters may be a pig, a mouse, a goose, a dog, or a duck. Sometimes her friends are sleeping, and sometimes they are playing. In some stories the hen bakes bread, and other times she bakes a cake. In all stories, the other animals never help, and the hen never lets them eat what she has baked.

Retold by Andrea Pelleschi

The Little Red Hen

Illustrated by Reggie Holladay

Once there was a Little Red Hen. She lived on a quiet farm. She liked to make tea and tend to her garden. A dog, a pig, and a cow lived on the farm, too. They liked to eat and sleep and lie in the sun.

One day, the Little Red Hen
found some grains of wheat.

"Look at this!" said the Little Red Hen. "We can make bread to have with our tea. But first we have to plant the grain."

"Who will help me plant the grain?" asked the Little Red Hen.

"Not I," said the dog.

"Not I," said the pig.

"Not I," said the cow. "We are too busy lying in the sun."

The Little Red Hen sighed. "Then I shall just have to plant the grain by myself." And that is exactly what she did.

The Little Red Hen planted the grain in neat rows. She watered it every day. Soon the wheat grew and grew and grew.

By the end of the summer, the wheat stood tall and golden. It was ready to be made into flour. But first it needed to be cut.

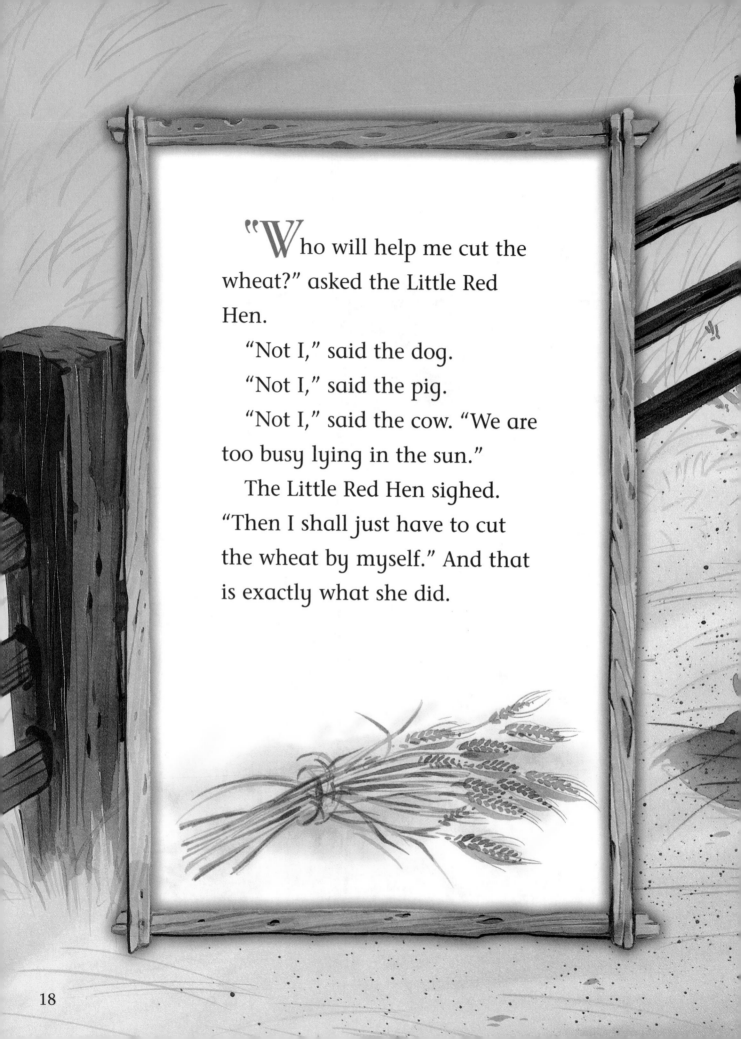

"Who will help me cut the wheat?" asked the Little Red Hen.

"Not I," said the dog.

"Not I," said the pig.

"Not I," said the cow. "We are too busy lying in the sun."

The Little Red Hen sighed. "Then I shall just have to cut the wheat by myself." And that is exactly what she did.

The Little Red Hen cut the wheat. Then, she tied it into bundles and shook loose all the grain.

The grain filled a wheelbarrow. It was enough grain for the miller to make flour. Proudly, the Little Red Hen showed the other animals.

"Who will help me take the grain to the miller?" asked the Little Red Hen.

"Not I," said the dog.

"Not I," said the pig.

"Not I," said the cow. "We are too busy lying in the sun."

The Little Red Hen sighed. "Then I shall just have to take the grain to the miller by myself." And that is exactly what she did.

The Little Red Hen pushed her wheelbarrow to the miller. The miller poured the grain into his mill. The mill turned round and round. It ground the grain into flour.

The Little Red Hen wheeled her bags of flour back to the farm. "Look at all this flour!" she said to the other animals. "Now we can bake the bread."

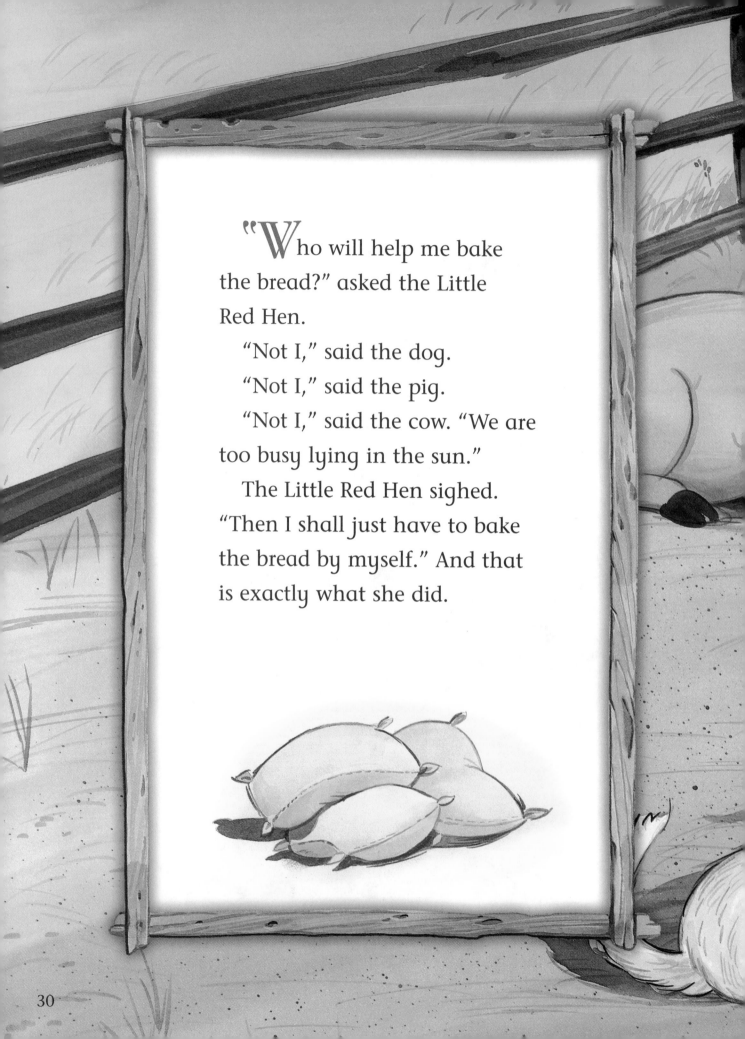

"Who will help me bake the bread?" asked the Little Red Hen.

"Not I," said the dog.

"Not I," said the pig.

"Not I," said the cow. "We are too busy lying in the sun."

The Little Red Hen sighed. "Then I shall just have to bake the bread by myself." And that is exactly what she did.

The Little Red Hen made dough. She mixed the flour with some water and yeast. After the dough rose, she put it into the oven to bake. Soon a wonderful smell filled the farmyard.

The bread turned golden brown. And the
Little Red Hen pulled the loaf from the oven.
Now, came her favorite part. It was time to eat
the bread.

"Who will help me eat the bread?" asked the Little Red Hen.

"I will," said the dog.

"I will," said the pig.

"I will," said the cow. "We are hungry from lying in the sun."

The Little Red Hen shook her head. "No, this time is different."

"You did not help me plant the grain," she told them. "You did not help me cut the wheat. You did not help me take the grain to the miller. And you did not help me bake the bread.

"All you did was lie in the sun. You are not going to help me eat the bread. I will eat all the bread by myself."

And with a nice cup of tea,
that is exactly what she did!

Bibliography
"The Little Red Hen"

Barton, Byron. *The Little Red Hen*. New York: HarperCollins, 1993. The author/illustrator uses his typical bold illustrations along with simple, repetitive text to make the story of the little red hen who plants the seeds, cuts the stalks, grinds the wheat, and bakes the bread a favorite for young readers.

Sturges, Philemon. *The Little Red Hen: (Makes a Pizza)*. New York: Dutton, 1999. The Little Red Hen decides to make a pizza, but first . . . she must go to the hardware store for a pan and to the supermarket and the deli for some necessary ingredients. This hen, however, does share with her idle neighbors, after which they help with the dishes.

Sathre, Vivian. *Three Kind Mice*. San Diego: Harcourt Brace, 1997. Three mice decide to surprise their friend the cat by baking him a birthday cake. The unsuspecting cat dozes, wakes, and seems to be about to pounce, but the mice manage to pull off their surprise despite occasional mishaps.

Min, Laura. *Mrs. Sato's Hens*. Glenview, IL: Good Year Books, 1994. In this engaging and colorful counting book, Mrs. Sato and a child count how many eggs the hens lay each day of the week.

Ada, Alma Flor. *The Rooster Who Went to His Uncle's Wedding: A Latin American Folktale*. New York: Putnam, 1993. There is no hen in this story, just a very hungry rooster who is dressed up and on his way to his uncle's wedding. The rooster spots a kernel of corn in the middle of a puddle and ends up with a muddy beak. He asks one character after another for help in this cumulative tale.

About "The Magic Fish"

"The Magic Fish" is a retelling of a tale that has been told in many different ways in many countries. In virtually all the versions, whether from Persia, Germany, India, China, France, or England, the main characters, through thoughtlessness or greed, waste three wishes that have been granted them. In some stories, the man wishes for pudding (sausages) to eat. Then, he wishes the pudding is on his wife's head and must use the third wish to remove the pudding from her head. In many European versions of the tale, the man is a woodcutter. These versions have no magic fish; instead they feature a fairy who grants three wishes to the woodcutter.

The first published appearance of the story in English was in 1761, and that version may have been taken from a French tale published in verse by the notable French scholar and storyteller Charles Perrault. However, the story had probably been told orally in Britain many years earlier.

Retold by Melissa Blackwell Burke

The Magic Fish

Illustrated by David Christensen

Once upon a time, there was a poor fisherman. He lived with his wife in a tiny hut by the sea.

Every day, the fisherman walked down to the sea. He fished all day long.

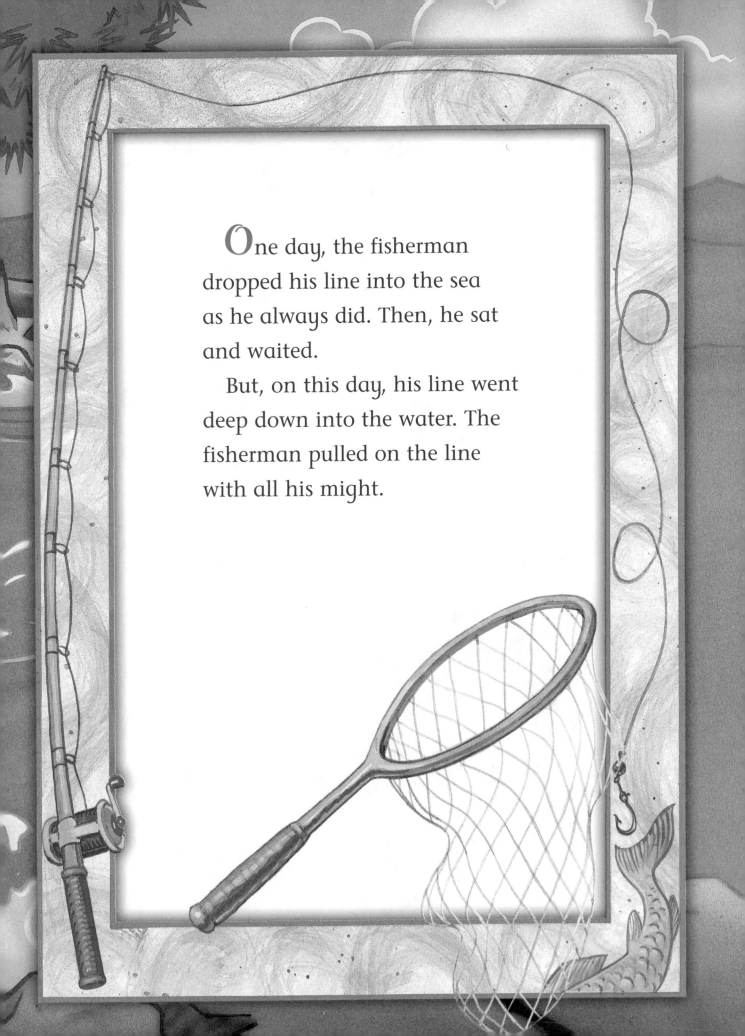

One day, the fisherman dropped his line into the sea as he always did. Then, he sat and waited.

But, on this day, his line went deep down into the water. The fisherman pulled on the line with all his might.

And, out of the water, he pulled a beautiful golden fish!

"Put me back in the water!" begged the fish. "I'm not a real fish. I am a prince under a spell. Please, let me go!"

"Yes, yes, of course," said the fisherman. "Of course, I'll let you go."

And, he threw the fish back into the sea.

Then, the fisherman went home.

"Was it a good catch today?" asked the fisherman's wife.

"You'll never believe what happened!" said the fisherman. "I caught a magic fish! He said he was a prince under a spell, so I let him go."

"A magic fish! Did he grant you a wish?" asked his wife.

"No," said the fisherman. "What would I wish for?"

"For a pretty little house, of course!" said his wife. "Go back to the fish. Tell him I want a pretty little house."

"I don't want to go," said the fisherman.

"Go!" said his wife.

So, the fisherman went back down to the sea.

The fisherman called out to the fish. The fish popped out of the water.

"Yes?" asked the fish.

"It's not me but my wife," the fisherman answered. "She wants a pretty little house."

"Go home," said the fish. "Your wife has it now."

When the fisherman got home, the hut was gone. And, in its place stood a pretty little house.

"Come and look," said the fisherman's wife. "Isn't this nice?"

"Very nice!" said the fisherman. "Now, we'll be happy."

And they were happy. They were happy for one week.

Then, the wife said, "This house is too small. Go back to the fish. Tell him I want to live in a big stone castle."

"I don't want to go," said the fisherman.

"Go!" said his wife.

So the fisherman went back down to the sea.

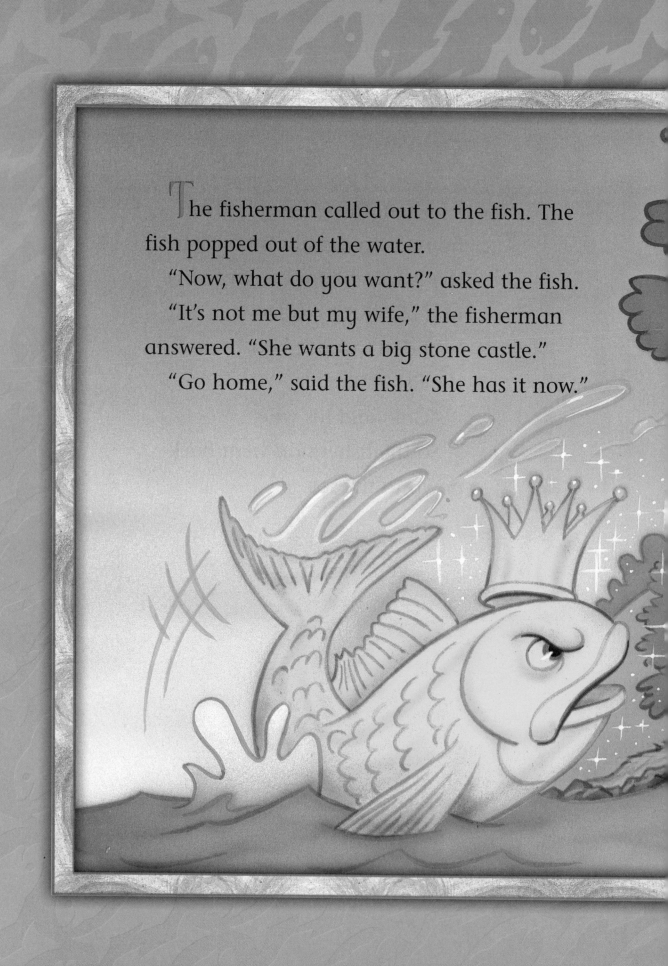

The fisherman called out to the fish. The fish popped out of the water.

"Now, what do you want?" asked the fish.

"It's not me but my wife," the fisherman answered. "She wants a big stone castle."

"Go home," said the fish. "She has it now."

When the fisherman got home, the pretty little house was gone. And in its place stood a big stone castle.

"Come and look," said the fisherman's wife. "Isn't this nice?"

"Very nice!" said the fisherman. "Now, we'll be happy."

And they were happy. They were happy for two weeks.

Then, the wife said, "Go back to the fish. Tell him I want to be queen."

"I don't want to go," said the fisherman.

"Go!" said his wife.

So the fisherman went back down to the sea.

The fisherman asked the fish. And the fish made the wife queen.

On and on it went. The wife was never happy. She always wanted something more. The fish granted each wish, but he was getting angry.

The fisherman thought that now his wife had everything she could ever want. But one evening, she surprised him.

"Go back to the fish," she said. "Tell him I want to make the sun and the moon rise."

The fisherman was shocked. "That is too much to ask!" he cried. "Be happy with what we have."

"Go!" said his wife.

So the fisherman went.

The fisherman called out to the fish. The fish popped out of the water.

"Well, what does she want now?" asked the fish.

The fisherman was nervous.

"She wants to make the sun and moon rise," he said.

"No!" said the fish. "Your wife wants too much. Go home. Now, she's back in the hut."

And so she was. And she's there to this very day.

Bibliography
"The Magic Fish"

Littledale, Freya. *The Magic Fish*. New York: Scholastic, 1985. This is a beautifully told version of the story of the fisherman's wife who is granted all her wishes but still is not satisfied.

Lewis, J. Patrick. *At the Wish of the Fish: A Russian Folktale*. New York: Atheneum, 1999. Unlike many fairy-tale characters who are granted wishes, the lazy man in this story knows how to use the wishes an enchanted fish promises him.

Dickens, Charles. *The Magic Fish-Bone*. San Diego: Harcourt Brace, 2000. In this tale, illustrated by Robert Florczak, a good fairy gives a magic fish-bone to a rather ordinary princess named Alicia. The only catch is that Alicia has to make her wishes at the right time.

Seuss Geisel, Theodore. *One Fish Two Fish Red Fish Blue Fish*. New York: Random House, 1981. The inviting rhymes and enchanting pictures of this classic Dr. Seuss story lend themselves to repeated readings.

Wu, Norbert. *Fish Faces*. New York: Henry Holt, 1993. This book introduces us to some fascinating underwater creatures, through simple text and more than seventy photographs the author has taken underwater.

About "Jack and the Beanstalk"

A print version of "Jack and the Beanstalk" first appeared in England in 1734, where it took the form of a skit in a book of "Christmas Entertainments." The skit is very silly, showing familiarity with the tale, but also making fun of it. Although it is primarily English, other versions of this tale appear in many countries, mostly in north-central Europe. It has also appeared among Native American tribes in Canada, apparently due to French tellings of the story there.

Like "Jack and the Beanstalk," many English fairy tales feature giants. And like Jack's giant, these other giants are always evil, have a good sense of smell, and can be very frightening. However, giants in the tales are always stupid, and the weakest person can outwit the most horrible giant. Some experts suggest that storytellers use giants in stories to show that intelligence is more important than size.

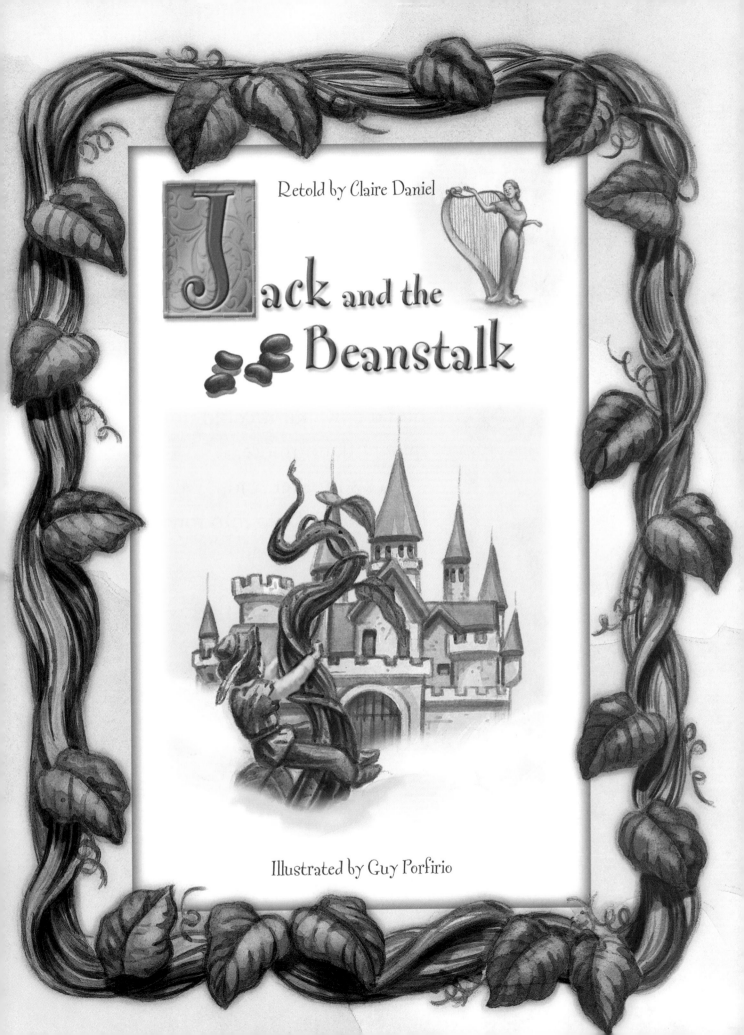

Retold by Claire Daniel

Jack and the Beanstalk

Illustrated by Guy Porfirio

Once upon a time, there was a boy named Jack. He lived with his mother. They had a cow, but it could not give milk anymore.

Jack's mother said, "We have no food. Go into town and sell our cow."

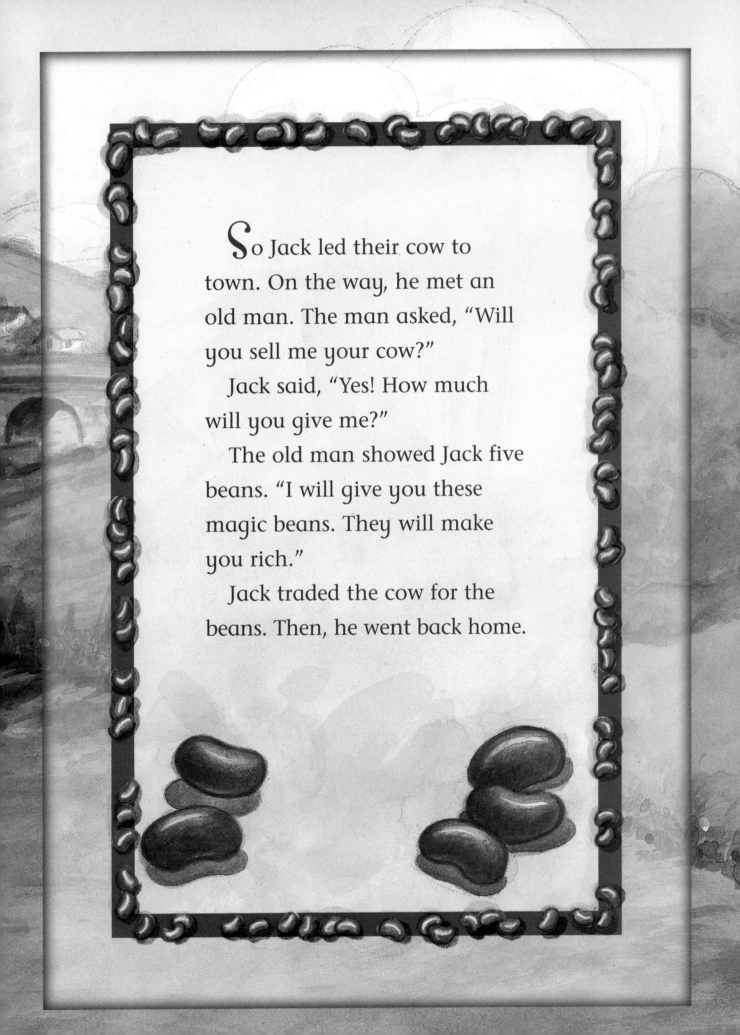

So Jack led their cow to town. On the way, he met an old man. The man asked, "Will you sell me your cow?"

Jack said, "Yes! How much will you give me?"

The old man showed Jack five beans. "I will give you these magic beans. They will make you rich."

Jack traded the cow for the beans. Then, he went back home.

Jack told his mother about the beans. But she was very angry. She said, "What have you done? Now, we have no cow and no money!"

Jack's mother threw the beans out the window. "There are no such things as magic beans. These beans are useless!"

The next morning, Jack looked out his window. He could not believe his eyes! The beans had grown into a tall beanstalk!

Jack loved to climb, so he climbed the beanstalk. He climbed and climbed and climbed. Jack climbed until he came to a castle in the sky.

Jack knocked on the castle door. A tall woman let him in. Jack said, "I have come a long way. I am hungry. Do you have anything to eat?"

The woman gave him some eggs. Then, they heard footsteps.

"Quick! Hide in the cupboard!" the woman yelled. "If my husband finds you, he will eat you up!"

Jack hid in the cupboard and waited.

A horrible giant came into the room.
He sniffed the air and said, "Fee, fi, fo, fum!
I smell the blood of an Englishman!"
His wife said, "No, sir! You smell
your breakfast."

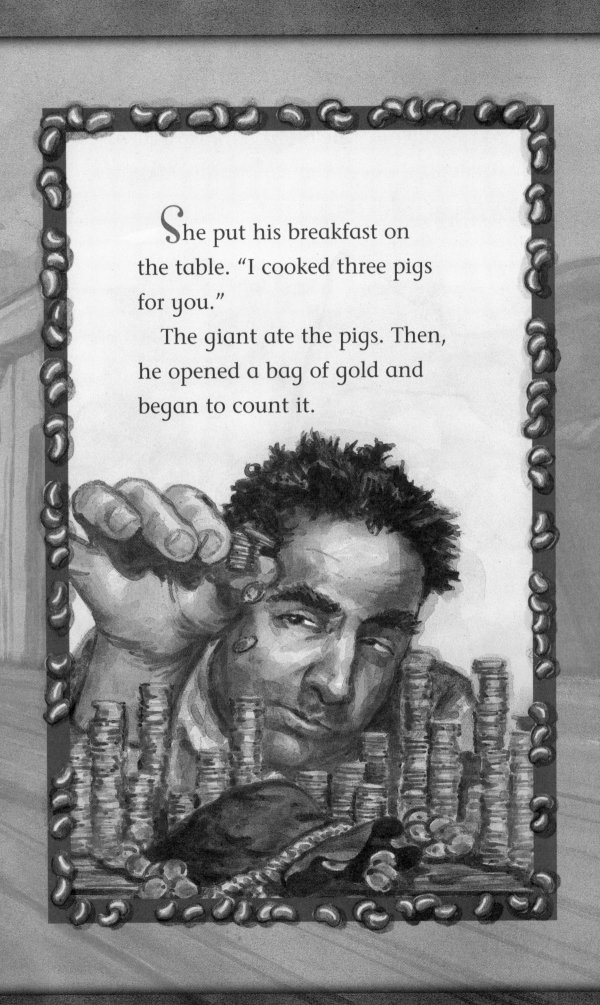

She put his breakfast on the table. "I cooked three pigs for you."

The giant ate the pigs. Then, he opened a bag of gold and began to count it.

After a while, the giant fell fast asleep.
Jack sneaked out of the cupboard. He grabbed
the bag of gold. He ran out of the house and
climbed down the beanstalk.

Jack's mother was very
happy to see the gold. They
had a lot to eat for a long time.

Then one day, the gold was gone. Jack decided to climb the beanstalk again. He climbed and climbed and climbed. Jack climbed until he came to the same castle in the sky.

Jack knocked on the door. The same woman opened it.

"Are you the boy who took our gold?" she asked.

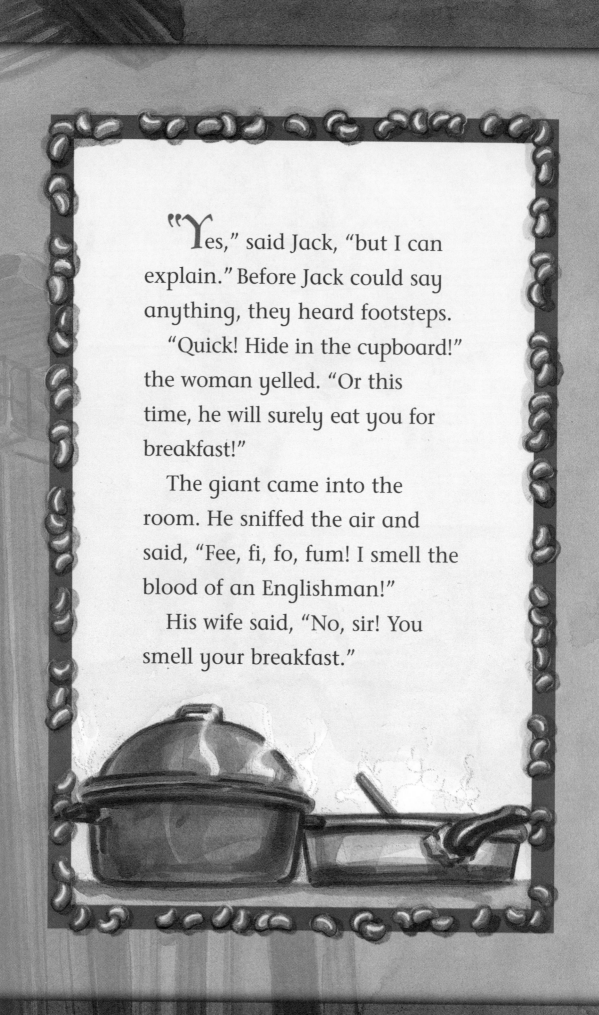

"Yes," said Jack, "but I can explain." Before Jack could say anything, they heard footsteps.

"Quick! Hide in the cupboard!" the woman yelled. "Or this time, he will surely eat you for breakfast!"

The giant came into the room. He sniffed the air and said, "Fee, fi, fo, fum! I smell the blood of an Englishman!"

His wife said, "No, sir! You smell your breakfast."

She put his breakfast on the table. "I cooked three cows for you."

The giant ate the cows. Then, he told the woman to bring him his hen.

She put the hen on the table. The giant said, "Lay!"

The hen laid a golden egg.

Soon, the giant fell fast asleep. Then, Jack sneaked out of the cupboard. He grabbed the hen and ran out of the castle.

Jack climbed down the beanstalk. He showed his mother the hen. "Lay!" he said, and the hen laid a golden egg. Jack's mother was very happy.

One day, Jack climbed the beanstalk again. He climbed and climbed and climbed. He climbed until he came to the same castle in the sky.

This time, Jack did not knock on the door. He sneaked inside the kitchen. Then, he climbed inside a tub and waited.

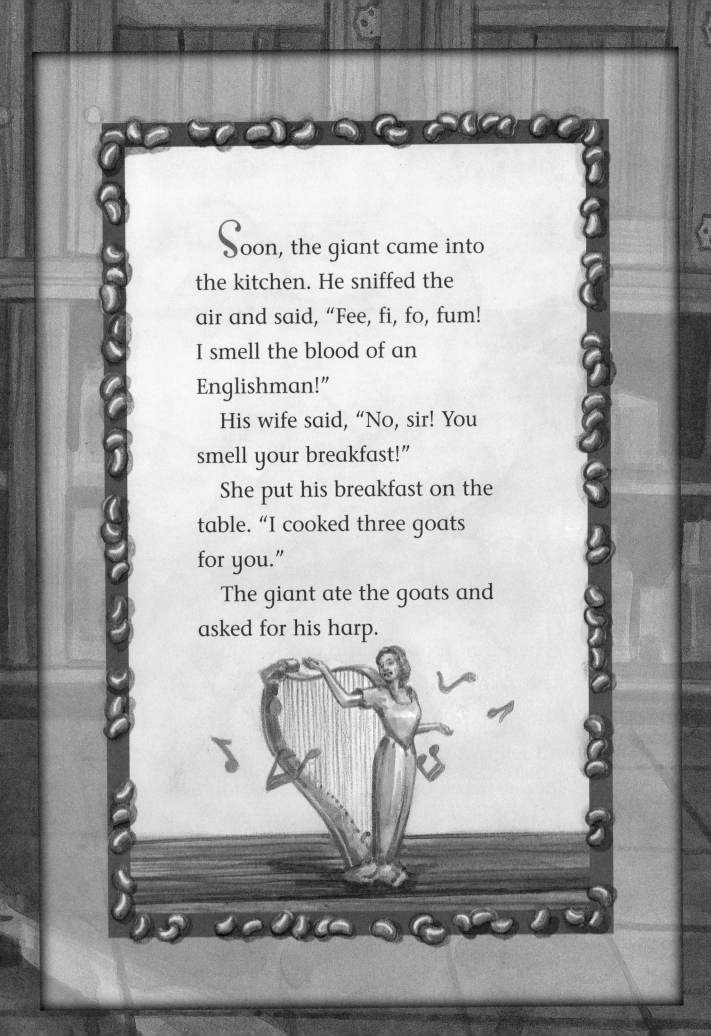

Soon, the giant came into the kitchen. He sniffed the air and said, "Fee, fi, fo, fum! I smell the blood of an Englishman!"

His wife said, "No, sir! You smell your breakfast!"

She put his breakfast on the table. "I cooked three goats for you."

The giant ate the goats and asked for his harp.

The woman put a harp on the table.

The giant said, "Play!"

The harp played beautiful music. Soon, the giant fell fast asleep.

Jack sneaked out of the tub. He grabbed the harp and ran. As he did, the harp cried out, "Master! Master!"

The giant jumped up and ran after Jack.

Jack climbed down the beanstalk as fast as he could. But the giant was right behind him! When Jack reached his house, he grabbed an ax.

CHOP, CHOP, CHOP!

Jack cut the beanstalk in two, and it fell down.

The giant fell down with the beanstalk.

BUMP! THUMP! THUD!

And that was the end of the giant.

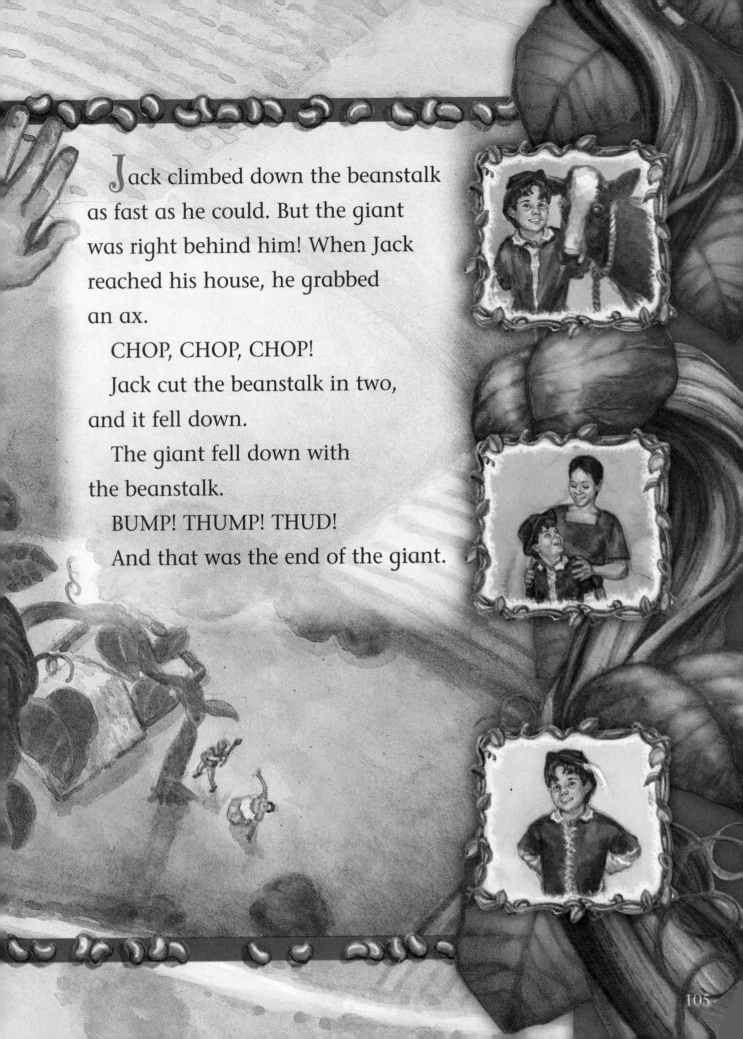

Jack and his mother were very happy. They had a hen that laid golden eggs. And they had a harp that played beautiful music. They lived happily ever after and were never hungry again.

Bibliography
"Jack and the Beanstalk"

Kellogg, Steven. *Jack and the Beanstalk*. New York: Morrow, 1991. Kellogg's whimsical illustrations and vivid text bring Jack's story to life. Jack is simple but not too simple, and the giant is scary but not too scary.

Brigs, Raymond. *Jim and the Beanstalk*. New York: Putnam & Grosset, 1997. Jim climbs a beanstalk, too, but instead of stealing from the giant he finds at the top, he helps the giant solve his very modern problems.

Demi. *The Empty Pot*. New York: Henry Holt, 1996. A Chinese emperor chooses his heir by giving seeds to each child in the kingdom to grow. All the children are able to grow flowers except Ping, who presents the emperor with an empty pot. The emperor's response teaches an important lesson.

dePaola, Tomie. *Jamie O'Rourke and the Big Potato*. New York: G. P. Putnam's Sons, 1992. Jamie O'Rourke, "the laziest man in all of Ireland," meets a leprechaun who gives him a magic seed that grows into a huge potato. The results are hilarious, but Jamie ends up as lazy as ever.

Ehlert, Lois. *Growing Vegetable Soup*. San Diego: Harcourt Brace, 1987. A father and child together plant seeds, water them, and watch the vegetables grow. When the vegetables are ripe, the father and child make a delicious vegetable soup. The soup recipe is included.

About "The Ugly Duckling"

"The Ugly Duckling" is perhaps the best-loved fairy tale written by Hans Christian Andersen, who believed that goodness and beauty would always win over evil.

Andersen was a storyteller who lived in Denmark between 1805 and 1875. He grew up in a simple household. His father was a poor cobbler, and the family had little money. Andersen was only 11 years old when his father died. Because he had such a difficult childhood, Hans Christian Andersen wrote many stories about people and animals who overcame poverty and unhappiness.

Retold by Claire Daniel

The Ugly Duckling

Illustrated by Loretta Lustig

ne fine spring day, a mother duck sat on some eggs in her nest. She wanted to keep the eggs warm. She sat quietly and waited for them to hatch.

The mother duck had five eggs in her nest. Four of the eggs were small. The fifth egg was very big.

Then one day, the eggs began to crack.
One, two, three, four small eggs hatched.
But the biggest egg did not hatch.

112

So the mother duck sat down again. She
kept the biggest egg warm. She waited for it to
hatch, too.

113

Finally, the big egg began to crack. The last duckling popped out.

"Cheep! Cheep!" he said.

The mother duck stared at the baby bird's long neck. She looked at his gray feathers. She looked at the other ducklings.

"He is not like the others," she thought. "But, he is my little duckling, and I love him very much."

The mother duck wanted to teach her ducklings to swim. She walked to the water. The four yellow ducklings followed her. So did the little gray duckling.

"What is that ugly thing?" said the other ducks at the pond. "Leave him alone!" the mother duck said. "He is my little duckling. He can swim. He is big and strong. He'll be a handsome duck one day."

But the ducks did not leave him alone. They hissed and pecked at him. They called him "the ugly duckling." So he decided to run away.

The ugly duckling swam up the river. There, he met some wild ducks.

But there were hunters nearby. They fired shots at the ducks. The ugly duckling was very frightened.

The wild ducks flew up and away. And the ugly duckling was alone again.

The ugly duckling swam on up the river.
Soon, he came to a cottage. He was very tired.
He lay down and went to sleep.

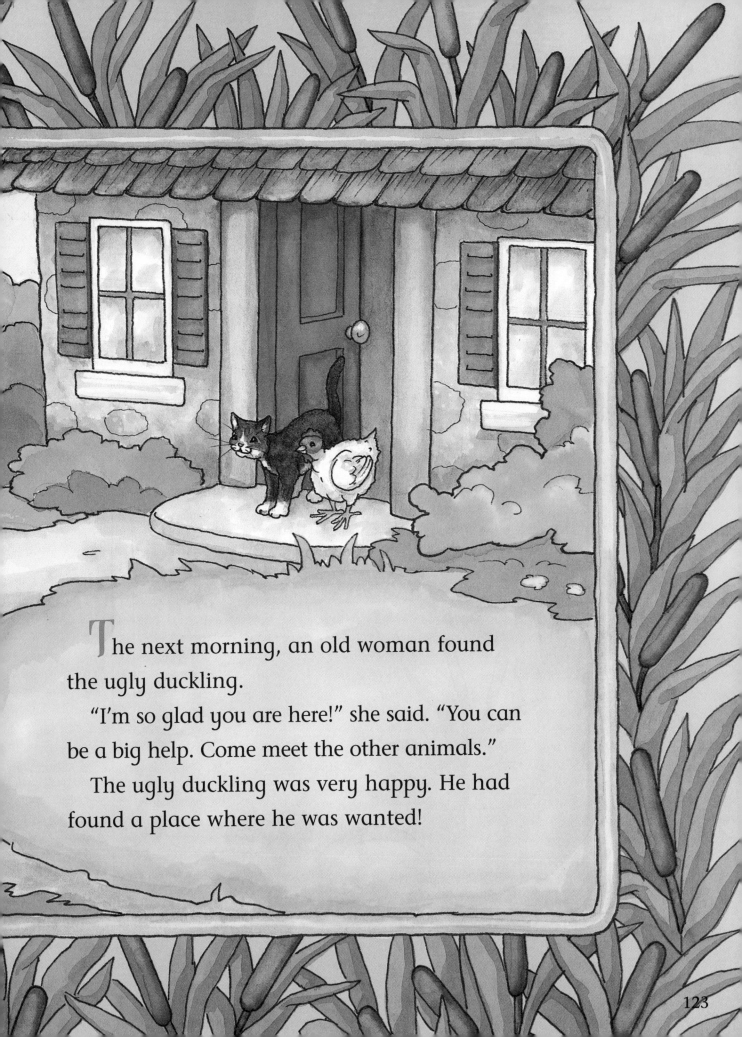

The next morning, an old woman found
the ugly duckling.

"I'm so glad you are here!" she said. "You can
be a big help. Come meet the other animals."

The ugly duckling was very happy. He had
found a place where he was wanted!

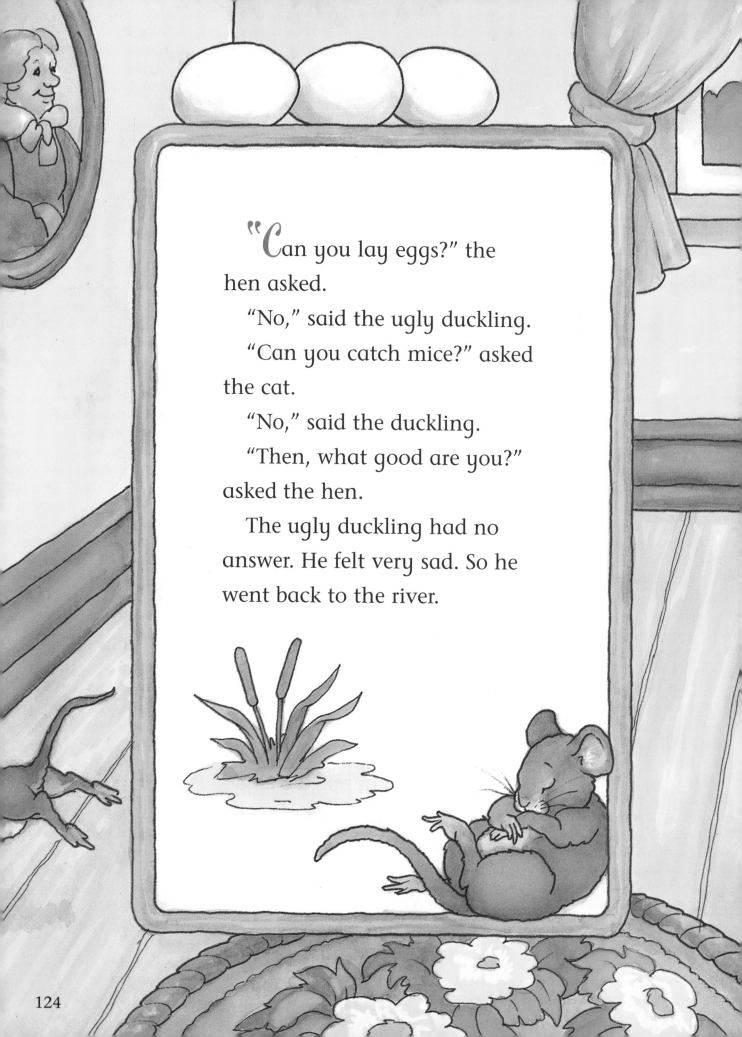

"Can you lay eggs?" the hen asked.

"No," said the ugly duckling.

"Can you catch mice?" asked the cat.

"No," said the duckling.

"Then, what good are you?" asked the hen.

The ugly duckling had no answer. He felt very sad. So he went back to the river.

The ugly duckling swam and swam. He caught fish to eat. He grew bigger and stronger. But, he was very lonely.

One day, the ugly duckling saw some beautiful birds in the sky. They were snowy white. They had long, slender necks. How he wished he could fly with them!

Winter came, and the ugly duckling found a small pond where he could stay. But, it got colder and colder. It snowed and snowed.

Then one day, the ugly duckling found that he could not swim. The pond had frozen. He was stuck in the ice!

130

A woodcutter saw the ugly duckling stuck in the ice. The woodcutter chopped away the ice. He took the duckling home.

The woodcutter put the duckling in front of the fire. Soon, the ugly duckling was warm and happy.

The next day, the ugly duckling felt better. But the woodcutter's children wanted to play. They chased the duckling all around the house until he flew out the door.

Many more days passed. The ugly duckling became cold and hungry.

Then one day, a warm breeze blew. Spring was coming! The ugly duckling looked up at the sky. He wanted to fly. So he raised his wings, and up he went.

As he flew, the ugly duckling saw some beautiful white birds down below. They were swimming in a pond.

The ugly duckling said, "How beautiful they are! I want to swim with them."

The ugly duckling flew down to the water. The beautiful white birds all came swimming toward him. The ugly duckling was frightened.

"Please don't hurt me," said the ugly duckling. "I know I am very ugly."

One of the birds said, "How could you be ugly? You are a swan! And swans are beautiful!"

The ugly duckling looked at himself in the water. He saw not an ugly duckling but a beautiful swan!

"Look!" cried a little girl from the shore. "Look at the new swan! He's the most beautiful one of all!"

The new swan raised his wings. All the children came to look at him.

The ugly duckling had been very unhappy. But, now he knew that he belonged with the beautiful swans. At last, he was very happy.

Bibliography
"The Ugly Duckling"

Andersen, Hans Christian. *The Ugly Duckling*. New York: Morrow, 1999. The rich, old-fashioned art, illustrated by Jerry Pinkney, is perfectly suited to the tale of the poor duckling who endures much loneliness and suffering before finally coming into his own.

McCloskey, Robert. *Make Way for Ducklings*. New York: Viking Press, 1941. It should come as no surprise that this book won the Caldecott Medal, awarded annually by the American Library Association to the illustrator of the most distinguished American picture book for children. This classic tells about a mallard family's search to find a safe home in the city.

Loomis, Jennifer. *A Duck in a Tree*. Owings Mills, MD: Stemmer House, 1996. Full-color photographs accompany the account of a pair of wood ducks as they migrate to Maine in the spring, mate, nest, raise their ducklings, and return to Florida for the winter.

Hest, Amy. *Baby Duck and the Bad Eyeglasses*. Cambridge, MA: Candlewick Press, 1999. Baby Duck gets glasses and cannot stand the way she looks in them. Thanks to her grandpa, Baby Duck soon changes her mind about her appearance.

Andersen, Hans Christian. *The Steadfast Tin Soldier*. New York: Harpercollins, 1992. This is a poignant, strikingly illustrated Anderson tale of a one-legged toy soldier who admires a paper ballerina from afar. It is retold by Tor Seidler and illustrated by Fred Marcellino.

About Aesop's Fables

Fables are very short stories that are told to teach a lesson. The story is not as important as what the reader learns from it. No one knows when the first fable was told, but Aesop is generally the best-known creator of fables. Lists of Aesop's fables include about 200 stories.

Aesop may or may not have been an actual person. Some people say he was a slave, and some say that he advised kings. Others say that "Aesop" is just an author's name that was invented to identify a certain kind of tale that used human-like animals to teach a lesson. If Aesop did actually live, it was probably in the 6th century B.C. Even if Aesop is just a legend, many people like to tell the stories that bear his name, because the lessons, or morals, still apply to everyday life.

Retold by Claire Daniel

Aesop's Fables

Illustrated by Kathleen McCord

The Hare and the Tortoise

Once, there was a hare who liked to brag. He liked to brag about how fast he was. Each day, he told the other animals, "I am so fast. I can run like the wind! Who will race with me?"

The other animals did not answer. They
did not like the hare's bragging. But no one
wanted to race with him.

One day, the hare said, "No one is faster than I am! Come on! Who will race with me?"

The tortoise was tired of hearing the hare brag. So, he said, "I will race you."

The hare laughed. "You must be joking!" he said. "You are so slow, and I am so fast. You will never beat me."

The tortoise said, "I may be slow, but I always get where I am going."

"We'll see about that," said the hare.

The next day, the hare and the tortoise were ready to race. All the animals came to watch. The goose waved a flag and shouted, "Go!"

The hare hopped away as fast as he could. Soon, he was out of sight.

The tortoise didn't think about how far ahead the hare was. He just inched along, step by step.

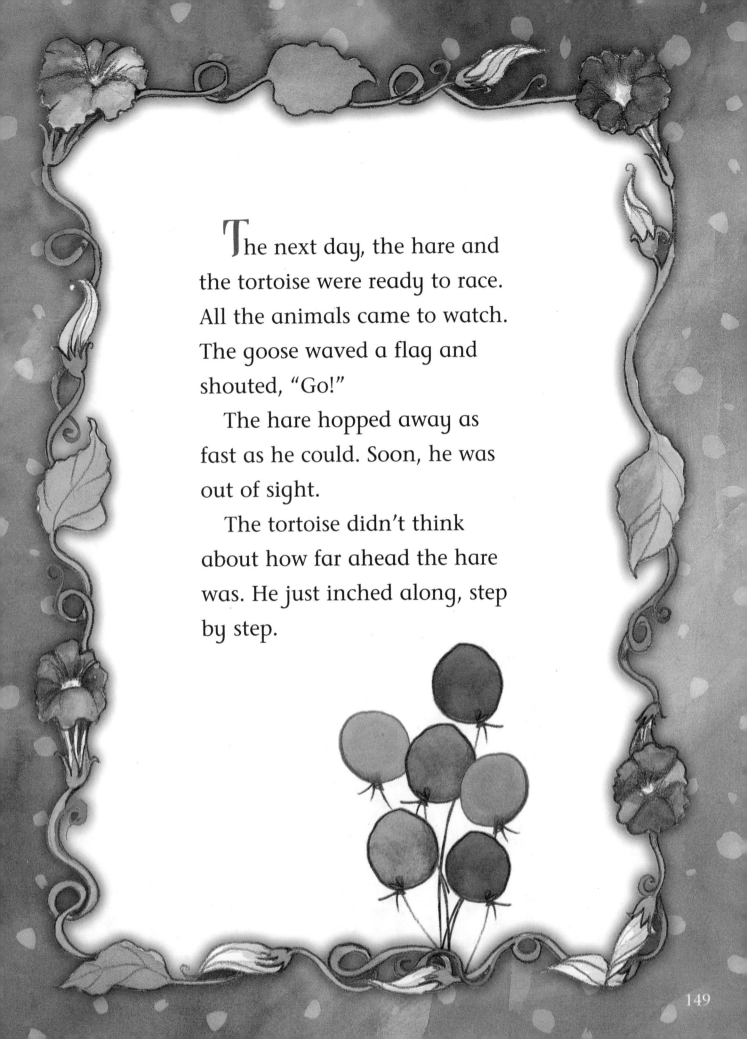

The hare ran and ran. After a short time, he got tired.

"The tortoise will never catch up with me!" he thought. "I'll just stop and take a little rest."

Soon, the hare was fast asleep. The tortoise was still walking. He walked slowly, but he never stopped.

As the tortoise walked, he passed the hare. But, the hare did not see the tortoise. The hare was still sleeping.

Suddenly, the other animals began to cheer. The noise woke the hare. He jumped up and ran as fast as he could. But it was too late. The tortoise had won the race.

The tortoise was happy. The other animals were happy, too. And, the hare had learned an important lesson:

Slow and steady wins the race.

The City Mouse and the Country Mouse

One day, a city mouse went to visit her cousin who lived in the country.

"I love it here!" said the city mouse. "I love the fresh country air!"

"I'm hungry after that long ride," said the city mouse. "Do you have anything to eat?"

"Follow me," said the country mouse. And she led her cousin to the garden.

The country mouse picked some ripe tomatoes. She picked corn, lettuce, and carrots, too. She shared the food with the city mouse.

"Here you are, cousin. Some nice, fresh country vegetables."

The city mouse looked at the vegetables.

"What kind of food is this?" she asked.

"This is what mice eat in the country," said the country mouse. "It's good for you."

"Come with me," said the city mouse. "I'll show you what mice eat in the city!"

So the city mouse took her cousin to the city.

Soon, they were in front of a big, fancy house. The city mouse took the country mouse inside. They saw a big table. It was filled with all kinds of food. There were cookies and cakes. There were pies and cheese and crackers.

The two mice ate happily. They ate and ate and ate until . . .

. . . in came two huge dogs!

The dogs jumped up on the table. They were not after the cookies and cakes. They were not after the pies and cheese and crackers. They were after the two mice!

The two mice ran into a little hole in the wall.

The city mouse said, "Wait a little while. The dogs will go. Then, we can eat again."

But, the country mouse said, "Not I! You can have your cakes and pies! I'm going home to eat my vegetables in peace."

It is better to eat a simple meal in peace than to have a feast in fear.

The Lion and the Mouse

One hot day, a lion fell asleep under a tree. A little mouse came running along. She scampered over the lion.

The lion woke up. He grabbed the mouse in his paw. The lion growled, "You woke me up! Now, I'm going to eat you!"

"Oh, no! I'm sorry I woke you," squeaked the mouse. "Please, don't eat me!"

But, the lion was not listening. He held the mouse over his mouth.

"Please, stop!" the mouse cried. "Do not eat me! I will help you one day."

The lion roared with laughter when he heard that. He was the king of the jungle, after all. How could a tiny mouse help him?

But the lion said, "Very well!" And he let the mouse go. The mouse ran away, and the lion went back to sleep. He forgot all about the mouse.

Not long after, some hunters caught the lion in a huge net. The lion roared. He tore at the net. Nothing helped. The lion was trapped.

The hunters saw what a fine lion they had caught. They went to find a wagon to carry him away.

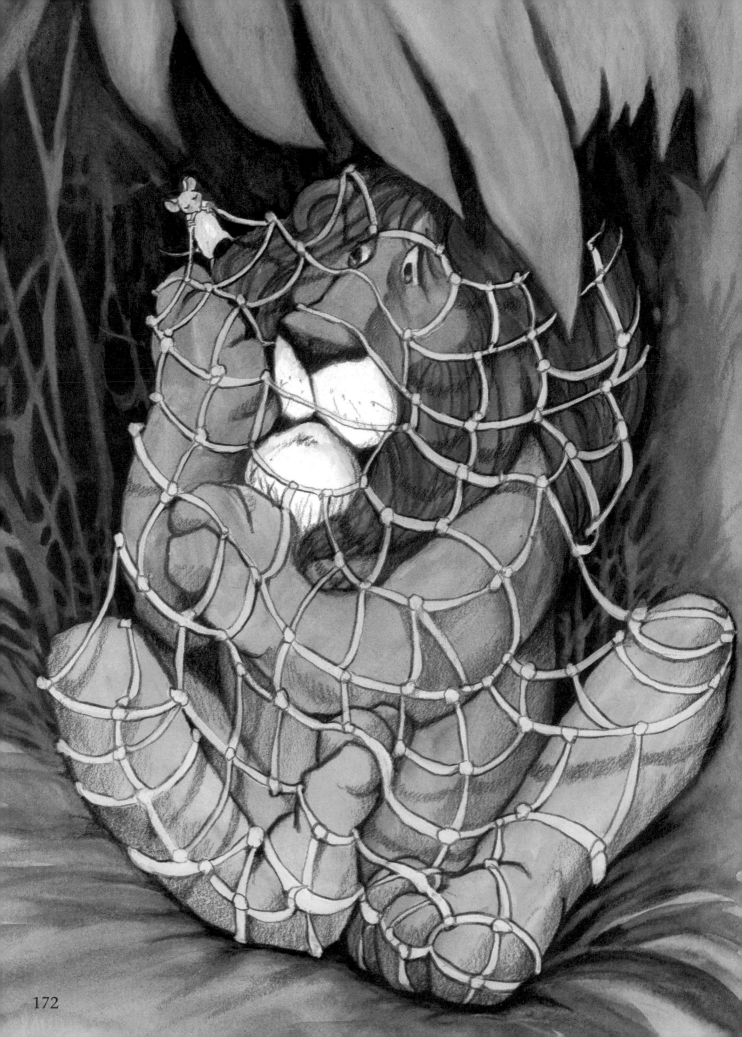

Just then, the mouse came out of hiding. She began to chew on the net. She chewed and chewed. Soon, she made a small hole in the net. Then, she made the hole bigger and bigger. All at once, the lion was free!

"Thank you!" said the lion to the mouse. "You saved my life!"

"I told you I would help you one day," said the mouse.

And from then on, the lion and the mouse became good friends.

Sometimes, small friends
can be big helpers.

Bibliography
Aesop's Fables

Aesop. *Aesop's Fables*. Selected and illustrated by Michael Hague. New York: Henry Holt, 1999. The language in this collection of fables is straightforward, but Hague's illustrations are rich in detail. His furry creatures, such as the hare, the lion, and the mice, look so realistic that the reader is tempted to stroke them.

Aesop. *The Tortoise and the Hare*. Adapted and illustrated by Janet Stevens. New York: Holiday House, 1985. The race is on between a boastful hare and a persevering tortoise in this retelling of the original Aesop tale.

Summers, Kate. *Milly and Tilly: The Story of a Town Mouse and a Country Mouse*. New York: Dutton Books, 1997. In this retelling of an Aesop tale, two friends, Milly and Tilly, discover that they lead very different lives, and each decides she prefers her own.

Aesop. *The Lion and the Mouse: An Aesop Fable*. Adapted and illustrated by Bernadette Watts. New York: North-South Books, 2000. Illustrated by Maggie Kneen, this simple retelling is set against an enticing jungle background.

Steig, William. *Doctor De Soto*. New York: Farrer, Straus, and Giroux, 1982. Unlike Aesop's lion, the fox in this charming story has difficulty overcoming his predatory nature while under the care of a dentist who happens to be a mouse. Never fear, though; Dr. De Soto and his wife are clever enough to meet the challenge.

About "Johnny Appleseed"

Yes, Johnny Appleseed was a real person. His real name was John Chapman, and he was born in Leominster (LEM-in-ster), Massachusetts, a small town where apple orchards grew in the countryside.

John Chapman had many younger brothers and sisters. Perhaps this made his family's home too noisy for John. He spent much time in the woods around his home, where he could be alone with his friends, the animals.

After Chapman left home as an adult, he never settled down. He bought land for his orchards, but never built a house, and he never married. He made friends with wild animals, pioneers, and Native Americans.

Chapman spent his life traveling, planting, and selling apple trees. If someone did not have enough money, Chapman would give the apple trees away. It was his dream for all the settlers who went out west to have all the apples they needed to begin a new life. Because John spent so much of his life planting and selling apple trees, he eventually became known as Johnny Appleseed.

Retold by Claire Daniel

Johnny Appleseed

Illustrated by CD Hullinger

It was a fall day more than 200 years ago. The leaves were orange, red, and yellow. The apples were ripe.

On that day, a boy named John Chapman was born in Massachusetts.

John grew up near the woods. He liked to play outside. He loved animals.

John went to school. He learned to read and write. He loved to learn new things.

When John was old enough, he worked in an apple orchard. He liked to feel the sun on his back. He loved to smell the rich, brown earth. But most of all, he loved the taste of fresh apples.

John had always wanted to go west. When he was a young man, John left home. As he walked, he carried a bag of apple seeds with him.

John walked for miles and miles and miles. It was warm, so he wore no shoes. He stopped at a river in Pennsylvania. There, John planted his first apple orchard.

John walked farther west. He planted more apple seeds along the way. John went back to his orchards many times. He took good care of his small apple trees.

Other people were also going west. They stopped when they saw John's apple orchards. John sold small trees to the settlers. They took the trees with them. They would plant them out west.

The settlers liked apples. In late summer, they ate apples right off the trees. In the fall, the settlers put apples in cellars. The cellars were cold and dark. The apples would not spoil there, so the settlers could eat apples all year round.

The settlers also baked the apples and cooked them in pots. They made applesauce and juice. They even fed apples to their cows!

John planted more trees. He walked and walked and walked. As he walked, John made many friends.

John loved to tell stories to the people he met. Children liked to sit around a fire and listen to his stories. So did grownups!

189

Each fall, John went back east to get more seeds. Then, he headed west again and looked for places to plant new trees.

In winter, John put fences around the orchards. He chopped firewood. He helped the settlers clear land.

John made friends with everyone. He
learned to speak with Native Americans.

Once, there was a fire. John's apple trees were in danger. The Native Americans helped him put it out. John's apple orchard was saved!

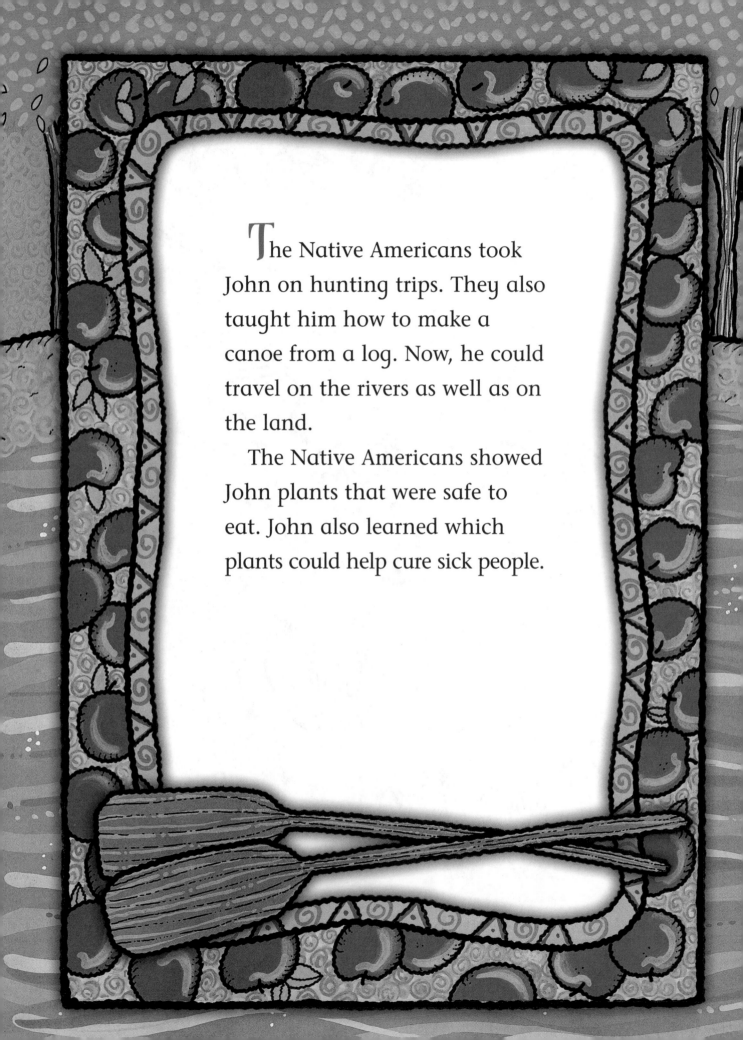

The Native Americans took John on hunting trips. They also taught him how to make a canoe from a log. Now, he could travel on the rivers as well as on the land.

The Native Americans showed John plants that were safe to eat. John also learned which plants could help cure sick people.

One day, the Native Americans and settlers fought each other. John knew that many people could be hurt. He told the settlers to go to a safe place. He helped save many lives that day.

John planted apple trees his whole life. He went to many different states. When he was 71, he was still planting trees.

One day, John walked a long way to one of his orchards. When he came back, he was very tired. He died a few days later.

After John died, people began calling him "Johnny Appleseed." They also told many tall tales about him. They said he played with a family of bears.

They said he saved a wolf's life. And the wolf became his pet.

People said John slept in trees. They said he talked to birds.

People said John never wore shoes. They said he walked in the snow in his bare feet.

People said a snake bit John on his foot. They said John didn't die because his feet were so tough.

People even said he wore a pot for a hat! People told all kinds of stories about Johnny Appleseed.

Are these stories true? Some of them may be. We don't really know.

We do know some things. Johnny Appleseed walked many miles. He walked across Pennsylvania, Ohio, Indiana, and even Iowa. He liked people and animals. And, he liked to help others.

And, we know one thing for sure—Johnny Appleseed loved apples. He brought apples to many places and many people.

Bibliography
"Johnny Appleseed"

Aliki. *The Story of Johnny Appleseed*. Englewood Cliffs, NJ: Prentice-Hall, 1963. Aliki offers her usual detailed illustrations and lively text in telling the legend of John Chapman, better known as Johnny Appleseed.

Glass, Andrew. *Folks Call Me Appleseed John*. New York: Doubleday, 1995. John Chapman was known to be a wonderful storyteller himself. In this delightful story, based on a real-life event, the author has Chapman narrate the tale of the time his half brother came to live with him in the wilderness.

Hutchings, Amy. *Picking Apples & Pumpkins*. New York: Scholastic, 1994. Beautiful photographs by Richard Hutchings help us follow a family's autumn outing. After the family picks the apples and pumpkins, we watch them carve jack-o'-lanterns and bake apple pies. The apple pie recipe is included.

Saunders-Smith, Gail. *Apple Trees (Plants Growing and Changing)*. Mankato, MN: Pebble Books, 1997. Photographs and simple text describe the changes an apple tree goes through from season to season.

Zagwyn, Deborah Turney. *Apple Batter*. Berkeley, CA: Tricycle Press, 1999. Loretta has never grown apples before; her 8-year-old son, Delmore, does not seem to be able to hit a fair ball. This is a beautifully told story of a mother and son who work hard toward meeting their separate goals. Yes, this one has a recipe, too, for apple crumble.

Reading Activities

The Puppets Tell the Story

Cut out the puppets below and on page 213. Glue them to craft sticks. Use the puppets to retell the story "The Little Red Hen."

The Little Red Hen

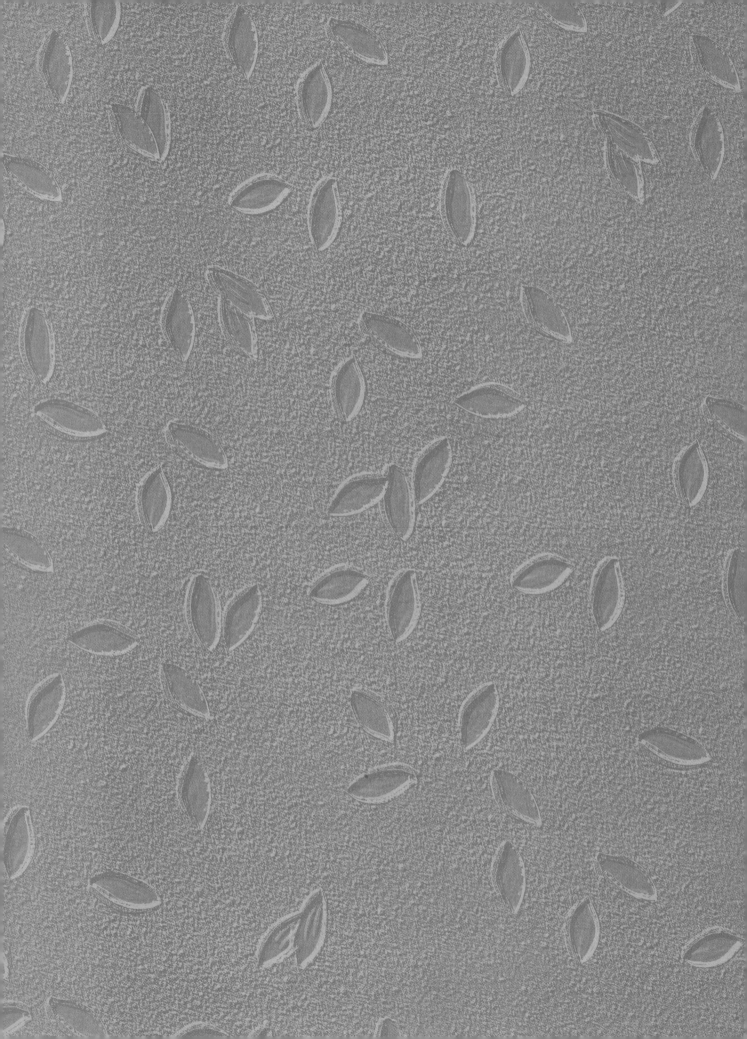

The Puppets Tell the Story (page 2)

The Little
Red Hen

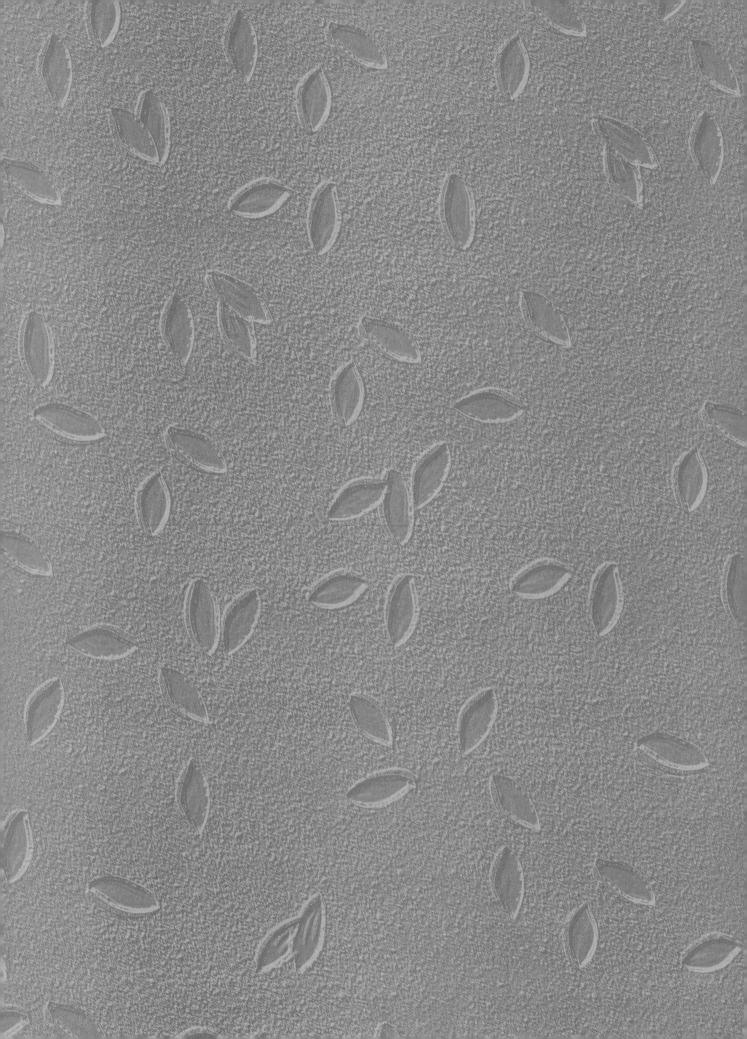

What Pays Off?

Look at each picture. Write the word in the blanks.
Hint: Check the story for spelling help.

The Little
Red Hen

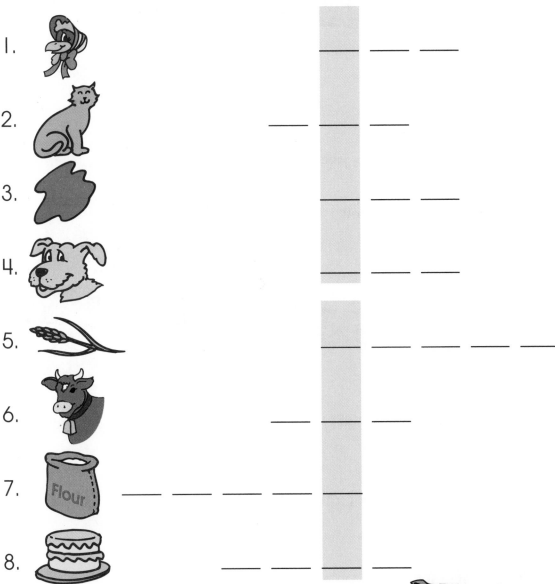

1. ___ ___ ___

2. ___ ___ ___

3. ___ ___ ___

4. ___ ___ ___

5. ___ ___ ___ ___

6. ___ ___

7. ___ ___ ___ ___

8. ___ ___ ___

Write the letters in the shaded box
from top to bottom on the lines
below to answer this question:
What does the little red hen say?

" ___ ___ ___ ___   ___ ___ ___ ___ pays off!"

Red Hen's Bread

Read the recipe. Then, write **Yes** or **No** after each sentence to tell about Little Red Hen.

The Little Red Hen

Ingredients

2 cups whole wheat flour

1/2 teaspoon salt

4 teaspoons baking powder

1 cup milk

Steps

Preheat oven to 375 degrees F.

Grease cookie sheet.

In a large bowl, mix flour, salt, and baking powder.

Add milk and stir.

Form dough into a ball.

Bake on a cookie sheet for 30–35 minutes.

1. Red Hen uses 2 teaspoons of salt. _____

2. Red Hen makes a ball of dough. _____

3. Red Hen puts the bread in the oven and then turns it on. _____

4. Red Hen greases the cookie sheet. _____

5. Red Hen adds milk and stirs. _____

Comprehension/Details

Who's Who?

Circle the words that tell about the characters.

The Little
Red Hen

Little Red Hen likes to	The other animals like to
make tea	make tea
sleep	sleep
garden	garden
lie in the sun	lie in the sun
work	work
eat	eat

Get That Wheat!

The Little Red Hen

The vowel sound in **wheat** is the **long e** sound. Color the wheat baskets yellow that show **long e** words. Then, draw a line to make a path through each colored basket from the wheat to the bread.

tea	eat	liked	end
hen	sleep	we	no
make	red	she	me
tend	smell	then	neat
be	need	wheel	yeast

Phonics/Long Vowel e

Learn to Read With Classic Stories—Grade 1

Tricky Words

Read the words in the list. Write one word to complete each sentence.

Hint: If you are not sure what the word is, find it in the story, and read the whole sentence.

Who

some

busy

was

one

_____

_____

1. Little Red Hen found _____ grain.

_____

_____

2. She _____ going to make bread.

" _____

_____

3. _____ will help me?" she asked.

_____

_____

4. Not _____ animal would help.

_____

_____

5. They were _____ lying in the sun.

One or More?

Nouns that mean **more than one** are called **plural nouns**. Many plural nouns end with **s**. **Hen** means **one**. **Hens** means **more than one** because it ends with **s**. Read the word in each box. Draw one picture if the word means one. Draw two pictures if the word means more than one.

The Little
Red Hen

bags	cow
pig	cups
pigs	oven

Read and Rhyme

Rhyming words have the same ending sound. Look at the picture, and read the word in the first column. Look at the picture in the second column. Change one letter in the first word to write the name of the second picture.

The Little
Red Hen

 hen

 10

_____

 dog

_____

 mill

_____

 hat

_____

 pup

_____

 barn

_____

What Do They Do?

The Little Red Hen

The Little Red Hen planted wheat and baked her own bread. But many people buy their bread in stores. Use the words in the list to complete each sentence to tell how people get their bread.

bakes   sells   plants

A farmer _____ the seeds.

A baker _____ the bread.

A grocer _____ the bread.

Word Meaning/Extending Vocabulary   **Learn to Read With Classic Stories—Grade 1**

Make a Book

Make your own book of "The Little Red Hen." Cut out the sentences below. Glue each one on a separate sheet of paper. Put the pages in order. Then, draw a picture for each page. Make a cover with the title on it. Now, read your book to a family member.

The Little Red Hen

"Who will plant the grain?"

"Who will bake the bread?"

"Who will cut the wheat?"

"I will eat the bread myself!"

"Who will eat the bread?"

"Who will take the grain to the miller?"

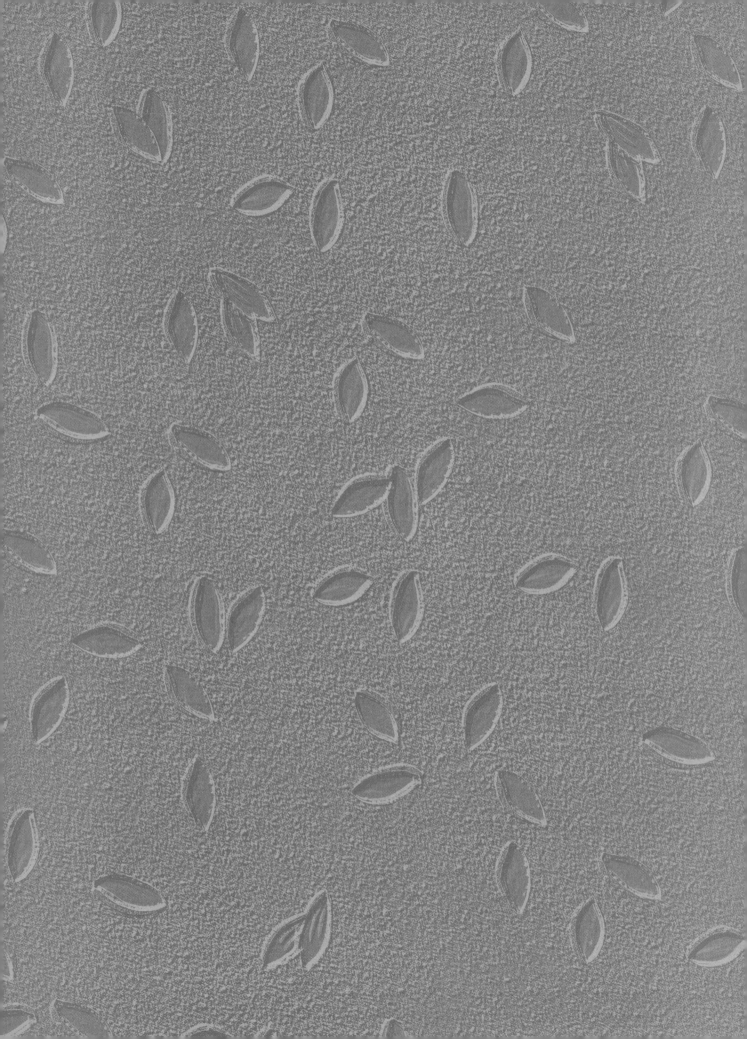

Around and Around

"The Magic Fish" is a circle story. At the end of the story, the characters are right back where they started! Cut out the pictures. Glue them in order on the story map on page 227. Then, retell the story. When you retell the story, you'll need to use the first picture twice.

The Magic Fish

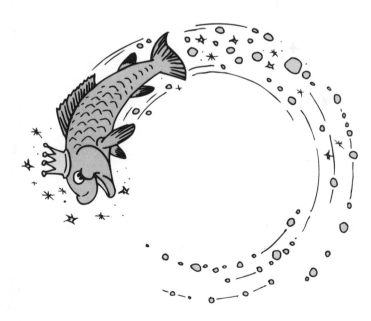

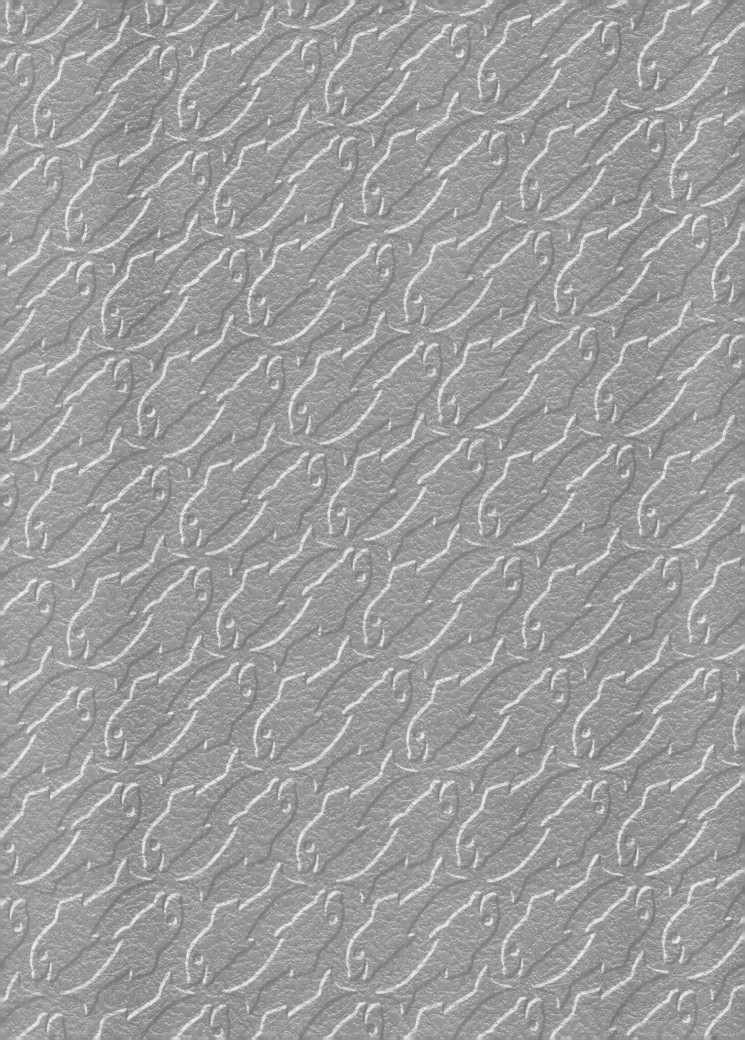

Around and Around (page 2)

The Magic Fish

1

2

6

3

5

4

Fish for a Word

Read the story words in the list. Write the correct word to complete each sentence.

queen
castle

enough

wish
hut

1. The magic fish gave the fisherman a _____ .

2. The fisherman's wife wanted to live in a _____ .

3. The fisherman thought one wish was _____ .

4. The fisherman's wife wanted to be a _____ .

5. The fisherman was happy in the _____ .

Word Meaning/Story Vocabulary

Learn to Read With Classic Stories—Grade 1

Catch Those Fish!

Short i is the vowel sound you hear in the word **fish**. The fisherman wants to catch fish that have the **short i** sound. Color the **short i** fish blue.

The Magic Fish

ride

pill

wish

hill

dish

pig

him

it

was

will

with

in

wife

How many blue fish did you catch? _____

Now, circle the words that rhyme with **hill**.

Draw a box around the words that rhyme with **fish**.

Tell Me More

Some words describe, or tell more about, other words. In the title "The Magic Fish," *magic* tells more about *fish*. Write a word from the list to tell more about the word under each picture.

pretty   stone   tiny   golden

_____ hut

_____ fish

_____ house

_____ castle

Grammar/Adjectives

Learn to Read With Classic Stories—Grade 1

Faces and Feelings

Look at the pictures from the story. Then, look in a mirror and make the same face. Draw a face in the circle to tell how the character is feeling. Use the feelings key below.

happy

angry

surprised

ashamed

Finish the Picture

Follow the directions to complete the picture.

1. Draw two real fish in the water.
2. Draw one golden fish in the water.
3. Draw three flowers on the bank.
4. Draw a hat on the fisherman's head.
5. Draw a bird flying in the sky.
6. Color the picture.

The
Magic Fish

Study Skills/Following Directions

Learn to Read With Classic Stories—Grade 1

Make the Sun Shine

A **long vowel** sound is the same as the vowel's name. Listen for long vowel sounds in **day**, **sea**, **time**, **go**, and **blue**. Read the words in the suns. If the word inside the sun has a long vowel sound, make it shine. Color it yellow.

Poetry Power

The Magic Fish

Read the sentences. Change the first letter in the underlined word to form a rhyming word that makes sense. Write the new word to complete the rhyme.

A man drank some <u>tea</u>
And walked down to the _____.

He fished all day <u>long</u>
While he whistled a _____.

He pulled with all his <u>might</u>,
And he saw a strange _____.

The man let the fish <u>go</u>.
He just couldn't say _____.

"I'll grant you a <u>wish</u>,"
Said the magic _____.

Unfinished Story

Write a word from the list to complete each sentence.
Use a word that has the same meaning as the word at
the beginning of the sentence.

The
Magic Fish

angry   happy   house   granted   sea

_____

ocean | 1. A fisherman lived by the _____.

glad | 2. The fisherman was _____ about what he had.

home | 3. The wife wanted a pretty little _____.

gave | 4. The magic fish _____ the wish.

mad | 5. The fish began to get _____.

Magic Contractions

The Magic Fish

A **contraction** is a way to write two words as one. An apostrophe (') shows where one or more letters are left out. **I'm** is a contraction. It stands for the two words **I am**. Read the contractions below. Write the contraction that can replace each pair of words.

I'll   isn't   we'll   he'll   he's

it's   she's   don't   aren't   you'll

he will _____   are not _____

is not _____   you will _____

he is _____   it is _____

I will _____   do not _____

we will _____   she is _____

A New Ending

Imagine that the story goes on. Read the new ending below. Then, write what you think the fisherman would say.

The castle was gone! The fisherman and his wife were back in the old hut. The fisherman went for a walk. He thought about what had happened.

All of a sudden, he heard a loud quack. He looked down and saw a duck. The duck was covered with mud. Its webbed foot was stuck in a vine. A little golden crown was nearby in the sand.

"Please help me," quacked the duck.

The fisherman helped the duck.

"Thank you," the happy duck said. He put on his crown. "I am a magic duck. Since you helped me, I will grant you one wish."

The poor fisherman said,

_____

_____

_____

_____

_____

The
Magic Fish

Three Magic Fish

Read this poem about three magic fish. Act it out using the movements shown.

Three magic fish
Went swimming out to sea.

The first one said,
"Can you swim as fast as me?"

The second one said,
"Just watch me dive and float."

The third one said,
"Here comes a boat!"

The men on the deck
Drop their lines with a plop.

Away the fish swim.
And do not stop.

Comprehension/Interpreting Text

Learn to Read With Classic Stories—Grade 1

Story Map

Cut out the pictures. Put them in order to make a story map. Use your map to retell the important events in the story.

Jack and the Beanstalk

Fee, Fi, Fo, Fum!

The words **fee**, **fi**, **fo**, and **fum** all begin with the sound of **f**. Say the name of the picture. If the name begins like **fee**, **fi**, **fo**, **fum**, write **f** to complete the word.

_____ ive

_____ an

_____ un

_____ ork

_____ ey

_____ eet

_____ ire

_____ ish

_____ ox

What Did They Say?

Look at the pictures. Read the sentences. Draw a line from the words to the character who said them.

Hide in the cupboard!

I have come a long way. Do you have anything to eat?

Go into town and sell our cow.

Fee, fi, fo, fum!

Will you sell me your cow?

Comprehension/Story Characters/Dialogue

Learn to Read With Classic Stories—Grade 1

Bean + stalk = Beanstalk

A **compound word** is two smaller words put together to make a new word. You can use the meanings of the two smaller words to figure out the meaning of the compound word.

bean   +   stalk   =   beanstalk

Cut out the pictures. Use them to make compound words. Check the colors on back. If they match, you have made a compound word. Then, draw a picture of each new word you make on page 245, and write the compound word on the line.

| coat | house | door | pan |
| bell | cake | rain | dog |

Jack and the Beanstalk

Jack and
the Beanstalk

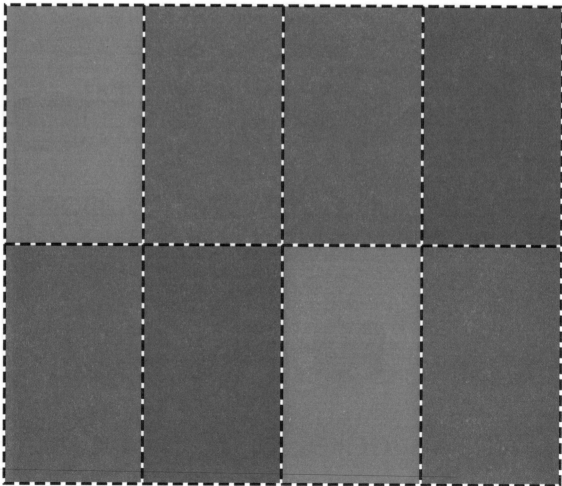

Word Structure/Compound Words

Learn to Read With Classic Stories—Grade 1

Bean + stalk = Beanstalk (page 2)

Jack and
the Beanstalk

Yes or No?

Read the questions. Circle **yes** or **no**.

Hint: Do you need help with an underlined word? Find the word in the story. Use the story and the pictures to figure out the word's meaning.

1. Did Jack and his mother live in a <u>castle</u>? **Yes** **No**

2. Did Jack <u>trade</u> the cow for beans? **Yes** **No**

3. Did Jack's mother think the beans were <u>magic</u>? **Yes** **No**

4. Did Jack <u>climb</u> the beanstalk? **Yes** **No**

5. Did the <u>giant</u> eat Jack? **Yes** **No**

6. Did the <u>harp</u> lay a golden egg? **Yes** **No**

7. Did Jack <u>sneak</u> into the castle? **Yes** **No**

8. Did Jack chop with an <u>ax</u>? **Yes** **No**

Vocabulary/Context Clues

Jack and the Beanstalk

All Mixed Up!

Look at the pictures in each row. Think about what happened **first**, **next**, and **last**. Then, number the pictures in the order in which they happened. Use **1**, **2**, and **3**.

Climb the Beanstalk

Help Jack climb the beanstalk! Color the leaves that have words that rhyme with **Jack** up to the giant's castle!

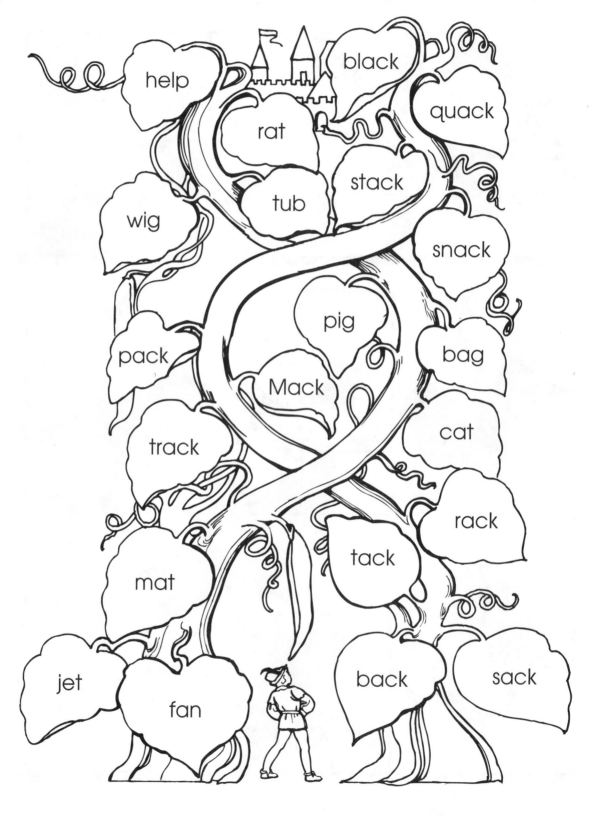

Phonics/Rhyming

Learn to Read With Classic Stories—Grade 1

Match the Opposites

The giant was big, and Jack was small. **Big** and **small** have **opposite** meanings. Read the words below. Draw lines to match the words with opposite meanings.

poor	happy
father	take
give	rich
angry	short
tall	mother

up	dinner
hide	down
breakfast	find
opened	awake
asleep	closed

What Is That?

Short a is the vowel sound you hear in **Jack**. Color the spaces with words that have the **short a** sound. What do you see?

Jack and the Beanstalk

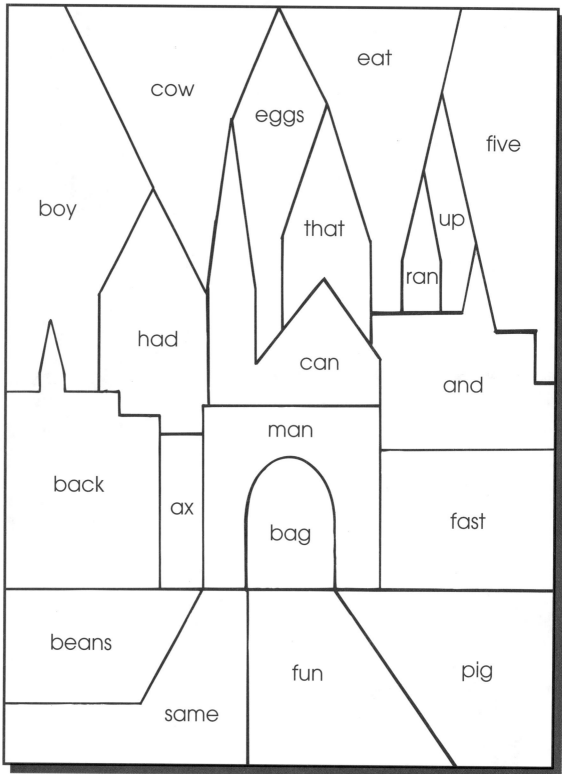

eat

cow

eggs

five

boy

that

up

ran

had

can

and

back

man

ax

bag

fast

beans

fun

pig

same

Learn to Read With Classic Stories—Grade 1

Order, Please

Read the words from the story. Underline the first letter of each word. Then, write them in ABC order.

cow   Jack   giant   harp

table   beans   mother   eggs

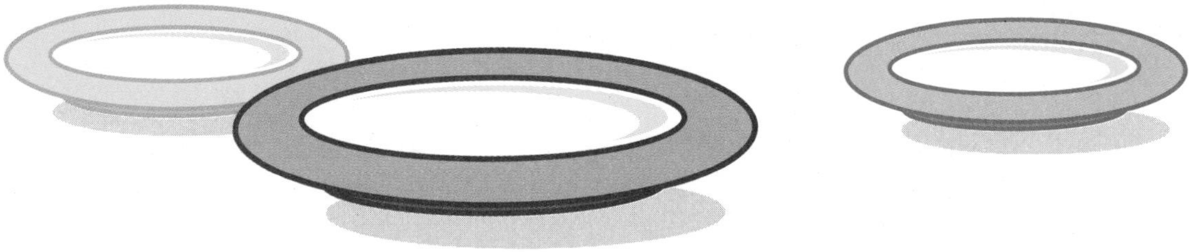

Jack and
the Beanstalk

1. _____   5. _____

2. _____   6. _____

3. _____   7. _____

4. _____   8. _____

Scrambled Sentences

A **telling sentence** begins with a capital letter and ends with a period. Write the words in order to make telling sentences.

1. magic the were beans

2. beanstalk Jack the climbed

3. took he the harp

4. woke giant the up

5. beanstalk cut the Jack

Mechanics/Capitalization and Punctuation   **Learn to Read With Classic Stories—Grade 1**

Sort It Out

Cut out the pictures below and on page 255. Put them in the correct order to tell the story of "The Ugly Duckling."

The Ugly Duckling

Sort It Out (page 2)

Cut out the pictures below and on page 253. Put them in the correct order to tell the story of "The Ugly Duckling."

The Ugly Duckling

D-D-D-Duckling

D stands for the beginning sound in **duckling**. Say the name of each picture below. If the name has the same beginning sound as duckling, write **d** on the line.

The Ugly Duckling

The Ugly Duckling

Name That Character

Draw a line to match each picture with the word or words that name the story character.

cat

old woman

ugly duckling

hen

woodcutter

mother duck

Word Meaning/Story Vocabulary   Learn to Read With Classic Stories—Grade 1

Tell Me Why

Match each sentence beginning with the correct ending. Write the letter of the ending on the line. The completed sentences will tell what happened and why it happened.

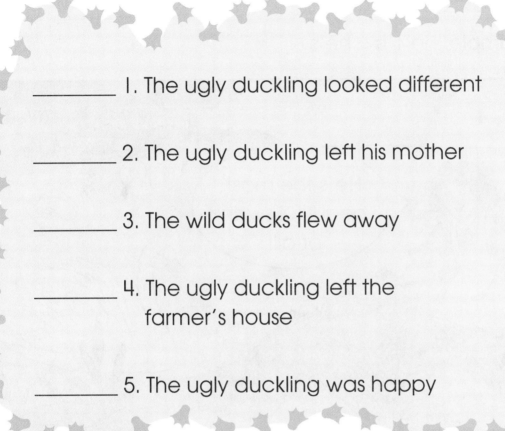

The Ugly Duckling

_____ 1. The ugly duckling looked different

_____ 2. The ugly duckling left his mother

_____ 3. The wild ducks flew away

_____ 4. The ugly duckling left the farmer's house

_____ 5. The ugly duckling was happy

a. because the children chased him.

b. because he wasn't really a duck.

c. because he had grown up to be a beautiful swan.

d. because hunters shot at them.

e. because the other ducks pecked at him.

Say It Another Way

The Ugly Duckling

The characters in the story "The Ugly Duckling" use contractions. A contraction is a short way of saying and writing two words. An apostrophe (') takes the place of the missing letters.

Example: he + is = he's

He's the most beautiful swan of all!

On page 261, read what each character says. Then, write a contraction from the list for the words in dark letters.

aren't	don't	He's
couldn't	I'm	You're

Say It Another Way (page 2)

"**He is** big and strong." _____

"**I am** so glad you are here." _____

"The duckling **could not** lay eggs." _____

"Please **do not** be mean to me." _____

"**You are** a swan." _____

"Swans **are not** ugly." _____

The Ugly Duckling

Action!

The Ugly Duckling

Verbs are words that show action. The words in the list are verbs. Write a verb from the list to complete each sentence.

wished

swam

hatched

snowed

pecked

1. Four small eggs _____ .

2. The ugly duckling _____ on the river.

3. The other ducks _____ at him.

4. He _____ he could fly with the swans.

5. In the winter, it _____ .

Opposites

The words **ugly** and **beautiful** have **opposite** meanings.
Read the story words in the first column. Draw lines to
match words with opposite meanings.

The Ugly
Duckling

happy ○	○ old
he ○	○ father
little ○	○ big
mother ○	○ sad
new ○	○ she
out ○	○ handsome
sat ○	○ down
ugly ○	○ cool
up ○	○ in
warm ○	○ stood

The Ugly Duckling

"Hatch" the Eggs

The **short e** sound is the vowel sound in **nest**. Say the name of each picture. If the picture name has the same vowel sound as **nest**, color the picture to "hatch" the egg.

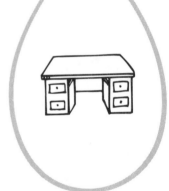

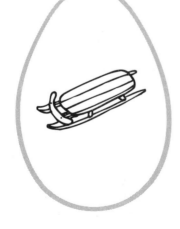

Phonics/Short Vowel e

Learn to Read With Classic Stories—Grade 1

Who Said That?

Cut out the pictures of the characters. Glue the pictures beside the words the characters said.

The Ugly Duckling

1. "I love my little duckling very much."

2. "You can lay eggs for us."

3. "Can you catch mice?"

4. "I know I am very ugly."

5. "The new swan is the most beautiful one of all."

Get It in Order

Cut out each set of pictures. Put them in the correct order. Retell each fable to a friend or family member.

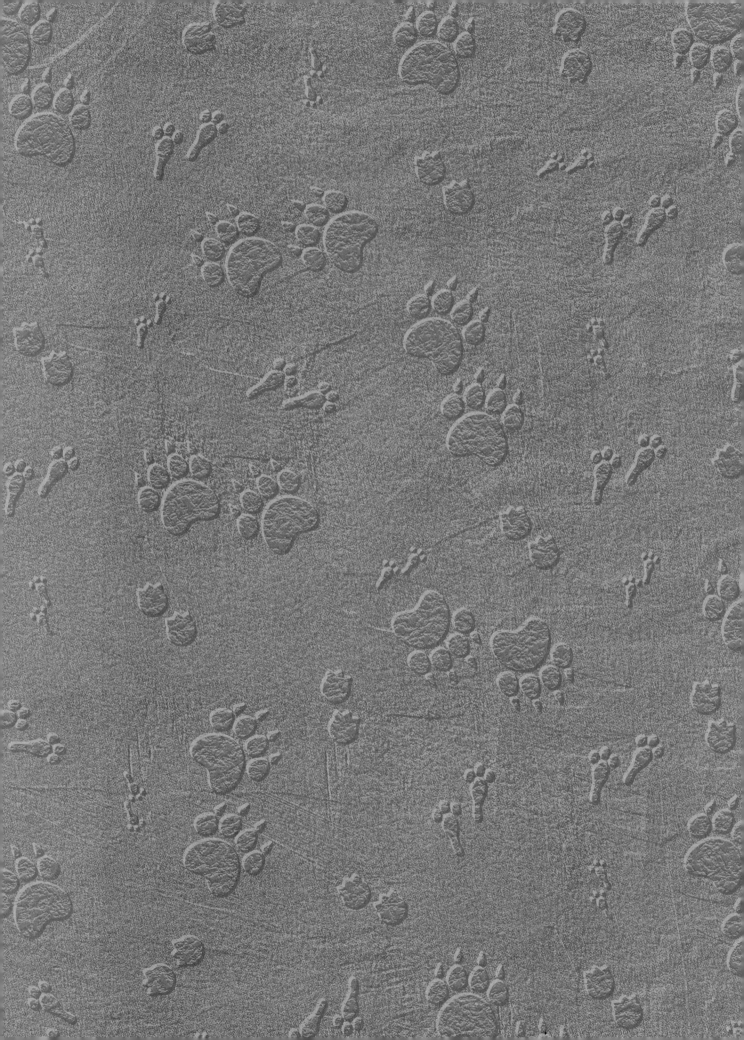

Story Words

Write a word from the list to complete each sentence.
Hint: If you need help reading a word, find it in the story. Reread the sentence the word is in.

One

Who

Come

again

could

Aesop's
Fables

_____

_____

1. _____ will race with the hare?

" _____

_____

2. _____ with me," said the city

mouse.

3. The country mouse was glad to be

_____

_____

home _____ .

_____

_____

4. "How _____ you ever help

me?" laughed the lion.

_____

_____

5. _____ day, the mouse did help the lion.

Write and Race

Put the words in alphabetical order to get the tortoise around the track. Work slowly and steadily. Don't wake up the hare!

Aesop's Fables

cheer   goose   slow   hare

wind   day   lesson   fast

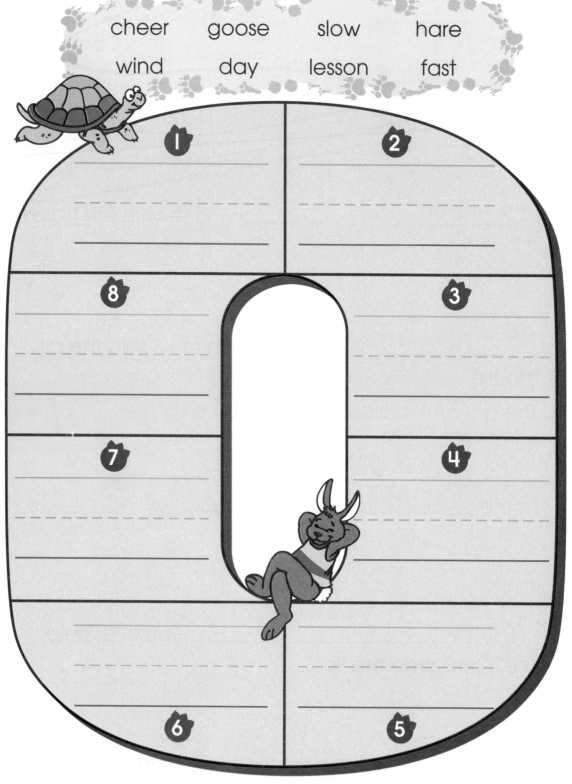

1

2

8

3

7

4

6

5

Study Skills/Alphabetical Order

Learn to Read With Classic Stories—Grade 1

Means the Same

Read the word that names the picture. Then, write a word from "The Hare and the Tortoise" that has almost the same meaning. If you need help, look back at the story.

rabbit

turtle

boast

quick

jumped

glad

Word Meaning/Synonyms

Aesop's
Fables

Vowel Sound Race

You can hear the **short a** sound in **brag**. You can hear the **long a** sound in **race**. Write the words from the list under the correct heading.

can   day   pass   flag   take

may   ran   fast   late   say

Short a Words

Long a Words

Phonics/Short Vowel a and Long Vowel a   **Learn to Read With Classic Stories—Grade 1**

Finding Her Way Home

One		More Than One	
goose		geese	
bear		bears	

Help the country mouse find her way home. Trace the path with words that mean **more than one**.

Word Structure/Plurals

Alike and Different

Read the words. Draw a line to the mouse the words tells about. If the words tell about both mice, draw a line to both of them.

Aesop's Fables

lives in a garden

has a cousin

eats cookies

eats vegetables

lives in a fancy house

is afraid of dogs

Comprehension/Compare and Contrast

Learn to Read With Classic Stories—Grade 1

A Meal for a Mouse

Mouse and **meal** begin with the sound of **m**. Say the name of each picture. If the name begins with the **m** sound, write **m** to complete the word.

_____ arrot	_____ ilk	_____ ake
_____ eat	_____ elon	_____ orn
_____ ie	_____ ints	_____ eese

Phonics/Consonant m

Lion and Mouse Sock Puppets

Make sock puppets of the lion and mouse. Use the puppets to retell the story.

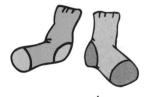

scissors

socks

glue

4 "wiggle" eyes
(optional—available in
craft and hobby stores)

yarn (optional)

What to do:

1. Cut out the parts of each animal on page 277. If you have the wiggle eyes, you do not need the paper eyes.

2. Glue the animal parts onto the socks. Let the glue dry.

3. If you want, add yellow yarn for the lion's mane. Add gray yarn for the mouse's tail.

4. Act out "The Lion and the Mouse."

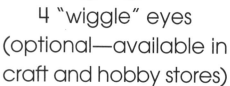
Aesop's Fables

Comprehension/Retelling

Learn to Read With Classic Stories—Grade 1

Lion and Mouse Sock Puppets (page 2)

Lion

Mouse

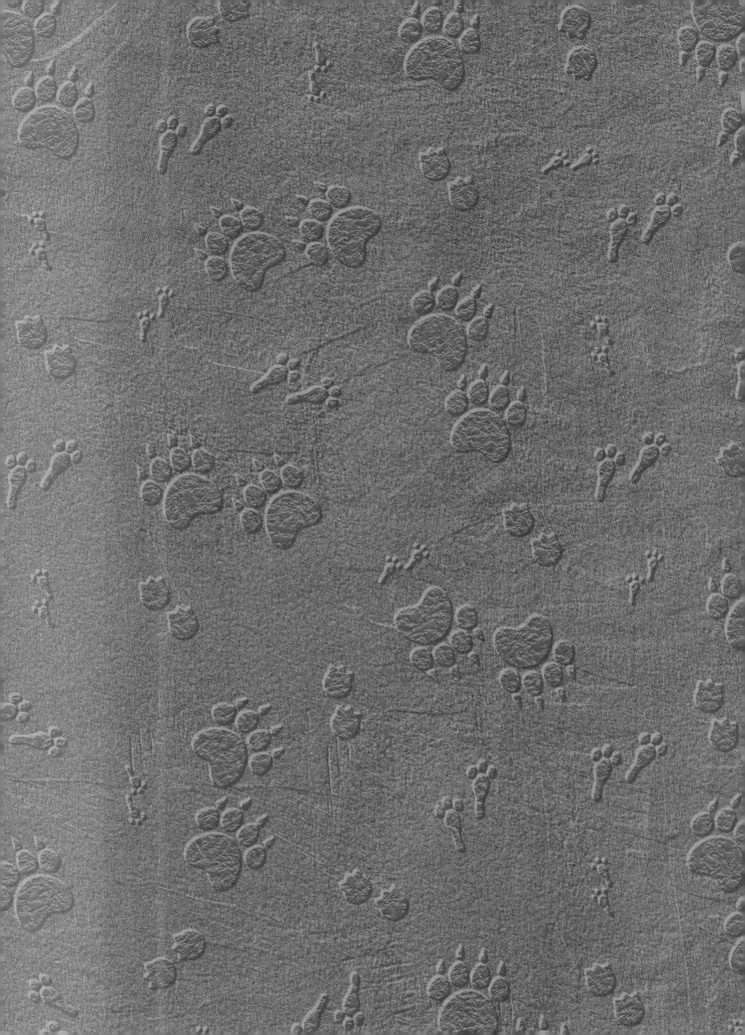

Story Sounds

Some words sound like what they mean. Write the word to tell the sound that is made in each picture.

Snap!

Honk!

Screech!

Meow!

Bang!

_____

_____

_____

_____

_____

_____

_____

_____

Aesop's Lessons

Read each story lesson. Then, draw a line from the lesson to the character who learned the lesson.

The Hare

The Country Mouse

The Lion

It is better to eat a simple meal in peace than to eat a feast in fear.

Sometimes, small friends can be big helpers.

Slow and steady wins the race.

Comprehension/Character

Learn to Read With Classic Stories—Grade 1

Map Johnny's Life

Read the sentences about John Chapman's life. Number the sentences to show the order in which they happened. Draw a line on the map to show where Johnny traveled.

Johnny
Appleseed

☐ Johnny spent his last days in Indiana.

☐ Johnny planted his first apple trees in Pennsylvania.

☐ Johnny was born in Massachusetts.

☐ Johnny planted many orchards in Ohio.

Minnesota

Wisconsin

Michigan

New Hampshire
Vermont

Maine

Massachusetts

New York

Rhode Island

Connecticut

Iowa

Pennsylvania

New Jersey

Ohio

Indiana

Delaware

Illinois

Maryland

Missouri

West Virginia

Virginia

Kentucky

Words and Pictures

Write story words from the list to label the pictures.

leaves   tree   bird

apple   log   snake

Word Meaning/Story Vocabulary   Learn to Read With Classic Stories—Grade 1

Noun Sort

Nouns are the names of people, places, and things. **Johnny** is a noun that names a person. **Orchard** is a noun that names a place. **Apple** is a noun that names a thing. Cut out the pictures below. Glue them in the correct column on page 285.

Johnny Appleseed

settler

canoe

fire

Native American

baby

river

Indiana

log

school

Noun Sort (page 2)

Sort the nouns. Glue each picture from page 283 in the correct column.

People	Places	Things

Johnny Appleseed

How Apple Trees Grow

Johnny
Appleseed

Look at the pictures that show how apple trees grow.
Draw a line from each picture to the sentence that tells
about it.

🍎 Plant some seeds.

🍎 Pick the apples.

🍎 Dig a hole.

🍎 Save seeds from
the apples.

🍎 Water the seeds.

🍎 Enjoy the blossoms.

Use the sentences and pictures to tell a friend or family
member how an apple tree grows. Explain how this
happens again and again.

Comprehension/Steps in a Process   Learn to Read With Classic Stories—Grade 1

Find the Way

Help Johnny Appleseed reach the river. Trace the path with words that have the **long e** sound you hear in the word **seed**.

Johnny
Appleseed

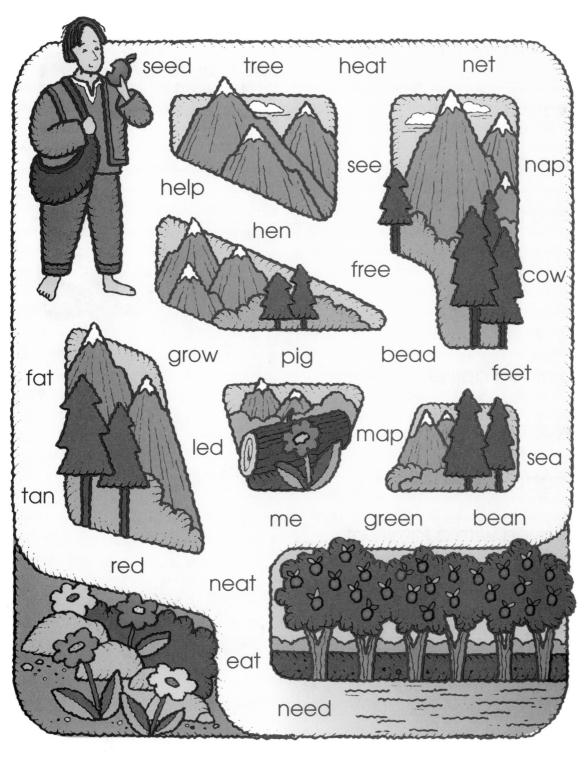

seed   tree   heat   net

help

see   nap

hen

free

cow

grow   pig   bead

feet

fat

led   map

sea

tan

me   green   bean

red

neat

eat

need

All About Johnny

Johnny
Appleseed

Write a word from the story to complete each sentence.
Write one letter on each line. Then, write the letters from
the shaded boxes in order on the lines below to complete
the last sentence. Look back in the story if you need to.

People said that Johnny . . .

wore a pot for a   ___ ___ ___ .

loved to eat   ___ ___ ___ ___ .

liked to help ___ ___ ___ ___ ___ ___ .

kept a pet   ___ ___ ___ ___ .

planted apple   ___ ___ ___ ___ ___ .

walked to ___ ___ ___ ___ ___ ___ .

made a canoe from a   ___ ___ ___ .

played with a family of ___ ___ ___ ___ .

walked barefoot in the   ___ ___ ___ ___ .

Some of the stories may be

___ ___ ___ ___   ___ ___ ___ ___ ___ .

A Pot for a Hat

People say Johnny wore a pot for a hat. **Pot** has the **short o** sound. Color the picture if its name has the **short o** sound.

The Ballad of Johnny Appleseed

Johnny
Appleseed

Rhyming words have the same ending sound. **Seeds** and **weeds** are rhyming words. Finish each rhyme by writing the letters to complete the rhyming word.

When John Chapman was a boy,

Apples were his favorite t ____ ____.

John left home as a young man.

He had some seeds and a good pl ____ ____.

Johnny walked for miles and miles.

He left behind both trees and sm ____ ____ ____ ____.

When you enjoy an apple tree,

Say, "Johnny planted this for m ____."

Phonics/Rhyming

Learn to Read With Classic Stories—Grade 1

Fix the Sentences

Hot and **cold** have opposite meanings. Read the sentences. On the line, write the opposite of the underlined word to make each sentence correct. Use words from the list.

many

west

summer

never

sad

1. _____ John walked <u>east</u> to plant apple trees.

2. _____ In late <u>winter</u>, apples were ready to eat.

3. _____ John was <u>glad</u> that his friends were fighting.

4. _____ People said John <u>always</u> wore shoes.

5. _____ Johnny Appleseed planted <u>few</u> trees.

Compound Words

A **compound word** is two smaller words put together to make a new word. **Appleseed** is a compound word. It is made from the words **apple** and **seed**. Cut out the apple halves on page 293. Put them together to make compound words. Then, write the words you make on the lines below.

Word Structure/Compound Words
Learn to Read With Classic Stories—Grade 1

Compound Words (page 2)

Cut out the apple halves. Put them together to make compound words. Write the words you make on the lines on page 292.

Johnny Appleseed

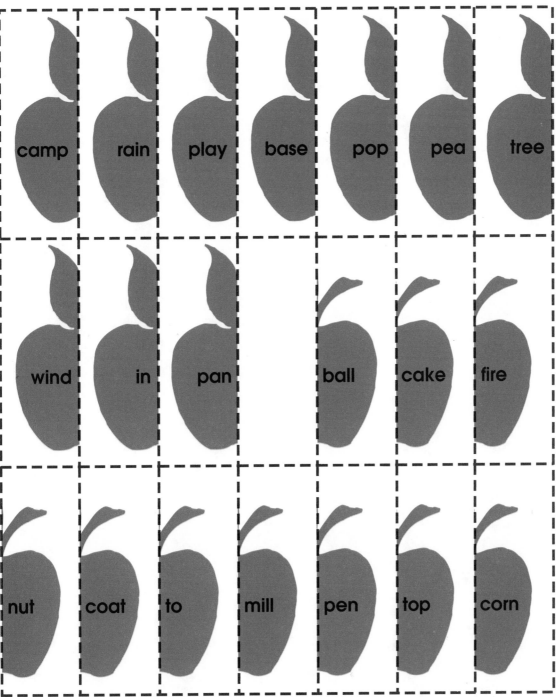

camp rain play base pop pea tree

wind in pan ball cake fire

nut coat to mill pen top corn

Reading Skills Checklist

Learning certain skills and strategies will help your child become a good reader. The following list shows the goals your child should reach in applying some basic skills during the first grade. Use the checklist after reading each story to assess your child's reading progress. Choose only a handful of skills to check at any one time. Sample questions have been given for each skill.

Skill	The Little Red Hen	The Magic Fish	Jack and the Beanstalk	The Ugly Duckling	Aesop's Fables	Johnny Appleseed
Cause and Effect Child recognizes that some actions or events can cause other events or results to happen. *Why did Jack hide in the cupboard? What made the giant chase Jack?*						
Classify/Categorize Child can sort similar things into groups. *Which animals can swim in this story? Which animals can't swim?*						
Compare and Contrast Child can tell how two things are the same and how they are different. *How is a duck like a swan? How is it different? What other animals are like ducks and swans?*						
Draw Conclusions Child can use information from a story and from real life to draw conclusions that are not stated in the story. *Why did Johnny Appleseed spend his time traveling?*						
Main Idea and Details Child can tell what a story is about and provide details. *What is this story mainly about? What steps does the little red hen take to make the cake?*						
Making Judgments Child can tell whether a character does something that is right or wrong. *Do you think the fish should have taken the wishes away? Why?*						
Phonics Child can identify most consonant and vowel sounds. *What word begins like* farm? *What letter makes this sound? What word has the same vowel sound you hear in* feet?						
Picture/Context Clues Child can use illustrations, sentence clues, and phonetic clues to help identify unfamiliar words in a story. *Look at the picture. What do you see that begins like* ball? *What did Jack climb? He climbed the _____. What do you do when you come to a word you don't know?*						

Skill	The Little Red Hen	The Magic Fish	Jack and the Beanstalk	The Ugly Duckling	Aesop's Fables	Johnny Appleseed
Predict Outcomes Child can tell what might happen next in a story. The prediction need not be accurate, as long as it is generally consistent with what has happened so far in the story. (during reading:) *What do you think will happen next in the story? Why do you think it will happen?* (after reading on:) *Did your prediction match what really happened?*						
Reality/Fantasy Child can tell whether a story could happen in real life or is make-believe, and can support the answer with a reason. *Could everything in this story happen in real life? What things happen that could not happen in real life?*						
Retell a Story Child can retell major events in a story in his or her own words. *What happened in this story?*						
Sequence Child can tell what happens first, next, and last in a story. *What happened first? after that? last?*						
Character Child can identify people or animals in a story and describe them. Child realizes that characters can be real or make-believe people or animals. *Who is in this story? Who is lazy in "The Little Red Hen"? Who is hard-working?*						
Plot Child can tell what happens in the beginning, middle, and end of the story. *How does this story begin? What happens next? How does this story end?*						
Setting Child can tell where and when a story is set. *Where does it happen? Is this a real or make-believe place? Did this story happen now or a long time ago?*						
Summarize Child can describe the important parts of a story. *Why did the hare lose the race? What did the tortoise do to win it?*						
Visualize Child can form a mental picture of what happens in a story. *Close your eyes. What do you see happening when the fish grants a wish?*						

Answer Key

215 — What Pays Off?

Look at each picture. Write the word in the blanks.
Hint: Check the story for spelling help.

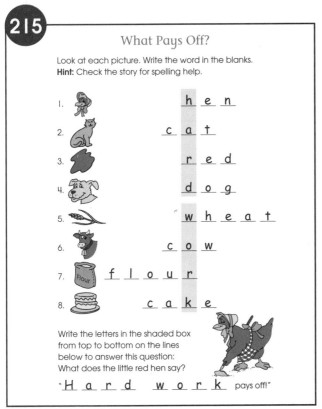

1. h e n
2. c a t
3. r e d
4. d o g
5. w h e a t
6. c o w
7. f l o u r
8. c a k e

Write the letters in the shaded box from top to bottom on the lines below to answer this question:
What does the little red hen say?

"H a r d   w o r k pays off!"

216 — Red Hen's Bread

Read the recipe. Then, write **Yes** or **No** after each sentence to tell about Little Red Hen.

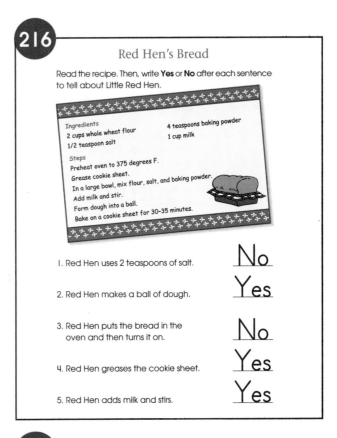

Ingredients
2 cups whole wheat flour
1/2 teaspoon salt
4 teaspoons baking powder
1 cup milk

Steps
Preheat oven to 375 degrees F.
Grease cookie sheet.
In a large bowl, mix flour, salt, and baking powder.
Add milk and stir.
Form dough into a ball.
Bake on a cookie sheet for 30–35 minutes.

1. Red Hen uses 2 teaspoons of salt. **No**
2. Red Hen makes a ball of dough. **Yes**
3. Red Hen puts the bread in the oven and then turns it on. **No**
4. Red Hen greases the cookie sheet. **Yes**
5. Red Hen adds milk and stirs. **Yes**

217 — Who's Who?

Circle the words that tell about the characters.

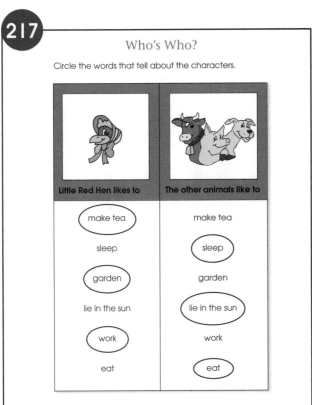

Little Red Hen likes to
- (make tea)
- sleep
- (garden)
- lie in the sun
- (work)
- eat

The other animals like to
- make tea
- (sleep)
- garden
- (lie in the sun)
- work
- (eat)

218 — Get That Wheat!

The vowel sound in **wheat** is the **long e** sound. Color the wheat baskets yellow that show **long e** words. Then, draw a line to make a path through each colored basket from the wheat to the bread.

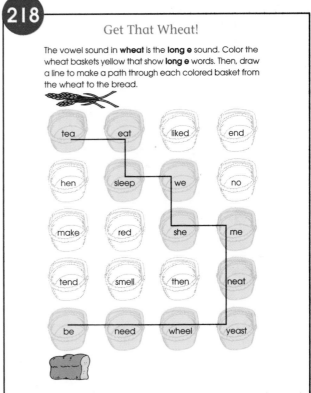

tea — eat   liked   end
hen   sleep — we   no
make   red   she — me
tend   smell   then   neat
be — need   wheel   yeast

219

Tricky Words

Read the words in the list. Write one word to complete each sentence.

Hint: If you are not sure what the word is, find it in the story, and read the whole sentence.

Who   busy   was
some   one

1. Little Red Hen found **some** grain.

2. She **was** going to make bread.

3. "**Who** will help me?" she asked.

4. Not **one** animal would help.

5. They were **busy** lying in the sun.

220

One or More?

Nouns that mean **more than one** are called **plural nouns**. Many plural nouns end with **s**. **Hen** means **one**. **Hens** means **more than one** because it ends with **s**. Read the word in each box. Draw one picture if the word means one. Draw two pictures if the word means more than one.

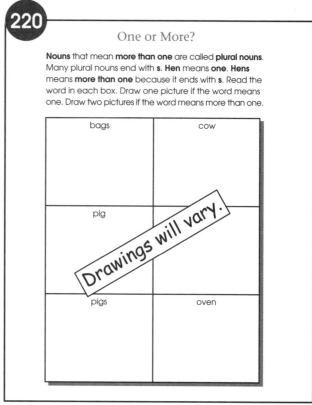

bags	cow
pig	Drawings will vary.
pigs	oven

221

Read and Rhyme

Rhyming words have the same ending sound. Look at the picture, and read the word in the first column. Look at the picture in the second column. Change one letter in the first word to write the name of the second picture.

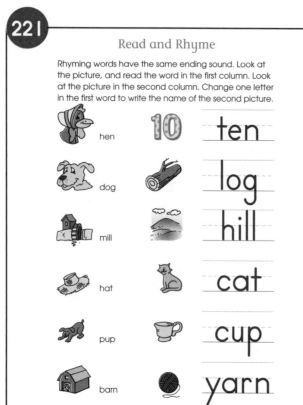

hen		**ten**
dog		**log**
mill		**hill**
hat		**cat**
pup		**cup**
barn		**yarn**

222

What Do They Do?

The Little Red Hen planted wheat and baked her own bread. But many people buy their bread in stores. Use the words in the list to complete each sentence to tell how people get their bread.

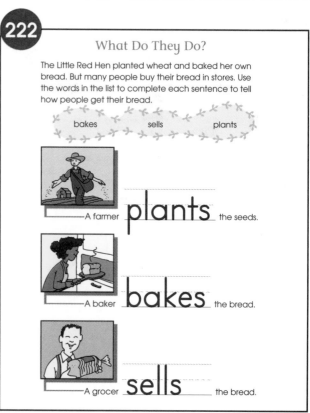

bakes   sells   plants

A farmer **plants** the seeds.

A baker **bakes** the bread.

A grocer **sells** the bread.

223

Make a Book

1   "Who will plant the grain?"

2   "Who will cut the wheat?"

3 "Who will take the grain to the miller?"

4   "Who will bake the bread?"

5   "Who will eat the bread?"

6   "I will eat the bread myself!"

227

Around and Around (page 2)

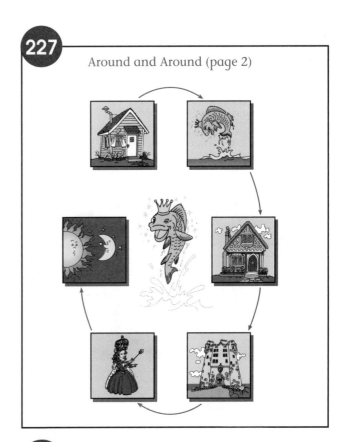

228

Fish for a Word

Read the story words in the list. Write the correct word to complete each sentence.

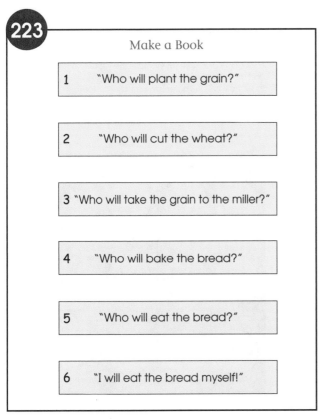

    queen   wish
    castle   enough   hut

1. The magic fish gave the fisherman a **wish** .

2. The fisherman's wife wanted to live in a **castle** .

3. The fisherman thought one wish was **enough** .

4. The fisherman's wife wanted to be a **queen** .

5. The fisherman was happy in the **hut**

229

Catch Those Fish!

Short i is the vowel sound you hear in the word **fish**. The fisherman wants to catch fish that have the **short i** sound. Color the **short i** fish blue.

How many blue fish did you catch? **10**

Now, circle the words that rhyme with **hill**.

Draw a box around the words that rhyme with **fish**.

230
Tell Me More

Some words describe, or tell more about, other words. In the title "The Magic Fish," *magic* tells more about *fish*. Write a word from the list to tell more about the word under each picture.

pretty   stone   tiny   golden

tiny hut   golden fish

pretty house   stone castle

231
Faces and Feelings

Look at the pictures from the story. Then, look in a mirror and make the same face. Draw a face in the circle to tell how the character is feeling. Use the feelings key below.

happy   angry   surprised   ashamed

232
Finish the Picture

Follow the directions to complete the picture.
1. Draw two real fish in the water.
2. Draw one golden fish in the water.
3. Draw three flowers on the bank.
4. Draw a hat on the fisherman's head.
5. Draw a bird flying in the sky.
6. Color the picture.

Colors will vary.

233
Make the Sun Shine

A **long vowel** sound is the same as the vowel's name. Listen for long vowel sounds in **day**, **sea**, **time**, **go**, and **blue**. Read the words in the suns. If the word inside the sun has a long vowel sound, make it shine. Color it yellow.

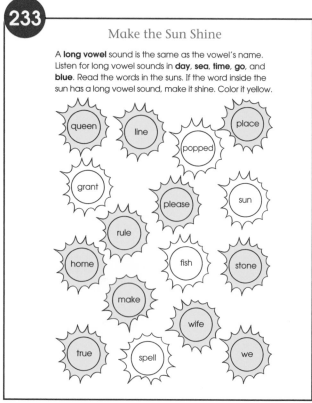

234 Poetry Power

Read the sentences. Change the first letter in the underlined word to form a rhyming word that makes sense. Write the new word to complete the rhyme.

A man drank some <u>tea</u>
And walked down to the _____ **sea** .

He fished all day <u>long</u>
While he whistled a _____ **song** .

He pulled with all his <u>might</u>,
And he saw a strange _____ **sight** .

The man let the fish <u>go</u>.
He just couldn't say _____ **no** .

"I'll grant you a <u>wish</u>,"
Said the magic _____ **fish** .

235 Unfinished Story

Write a word from the list to complete each sentence. Use a word that has the same meaning as the word at the beginning of the sentence.

angry   happy   house   granted   sea

ocean	1. A fisherman lived by the **sea** .
glad	2. The fisherman was **happy** about what he had.
home	3. The wife wanted a pretty little **house** .
gave	4. The magic fish **granted** the wish.
mad	5. The fish began to get **angry**

236 Magic Contractions

A **contraction** is a way to write two words as one. An apostrophe (') shows where one or more letters are left out. **I'm** is a contraction. It stands for the two words **I am**. Read the contractions below. Write the contraction that can replace each pair of words.

I'll   isn't   we'll   he'll   he's
it's   she's   don't   aren't   you'll

he will	**he'll**	are not	**aren't**
is not	**isn't**	you will	**you'll**
he is	**he's**	it is	**it's**
I will	**I'll**	do not	**don't**
we will	**we'll**	she is	**she's**

237 A New Ending

Imagine that the story goes on. Read the new ending below. Then, write what you think the fisherman would say.

The castle was gone! The fisherman and his wife were back in the old hut. The fisherman went for a walk. He thought about what had happened.

All of a sudden, he heard a loud quack. He looked down and saw a duck. The duck was covered with mud. Its webbed foot was stuck in a vine. A little golden crown was nearby in the sand.

"Please help me," quacked the duck.

The fisherman helped the duck.

"Thank you," the happy duck said. He put on his crown. "I am a magic duck. Since you helped me, I will grant you one wish."

The poor fisherman said,

Answers will vary. Sample Answer:
"No, thank you. I've had enough. Wishes are more trouble than they're worth."
And he never even told his wife about the magic duck.

239

Story Map

Cut out the pictures. Put them in order to make a story map. Use your map to retell the important events in the story.

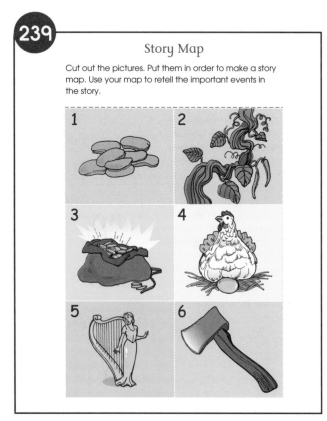

241

Fee, Fi, Fo, Fum!

The words **fee**, **fi**, **fo**, and **fum** all begin with the sound of **f**. Say the name of the picture. If the name begins like **fee, fi, fo, fum**, write **f** to complete the word.

242

What Did They Say?

Look at the pictures. Read the sentences. Draw a line from the words to the character who said them.

243

Bean + stalk = Beanstalk

245

Bean + stalk = Beanstalk (page 2)

Drawing will vary.	Drawing will vary.
raincoat	doorbell
Drawing will vary.	Drawing will vary.
pancake	doghouse

246

Yes or No?

Read the questions. Circle **yes** or **no**.

Hint: Do you need help with an underlined word? Find the word in the story. Use the story and the pictures to figure out the word's meaning.

1. Did Jack and his mother live in a <u>castle</u>?   Yes   (No)

2. Did Jack <u>trade</u> the cow for beans?   (Yes)   No

3. Did Jack's mother think the beans were <u>magic</u>?   Yes   (No)

4. Did Jack <u>climb</u> the beanstalk?   (Yes)   No

5. Did the <u>giant</u> eat Jack?   Yes   (No)

6. Did the <u>harp</u> lay a golden egg?   Yes   (No)

7. Did Jack <u>sneak</u> into the castle?   (Yes)   No

8. Did Jack chop with an <u>ax</u>?   (Yes)   No

247

All Mixed Up!

Look at the pictures in each row. Think about what happened **first**, **next**, and **last**. Then, number the pictures in the order in which they happened. Use **1**, **2**, and **3**.

Row 1: 2, 1, 3
Row 2: 3, 1, 2
Row 3: 1, 3, 2

248

Climb the Beanstalk

Help Jack climb the beanstalk! Color the leaves that have words that rhyme with **Jack** up to the giant's castle!

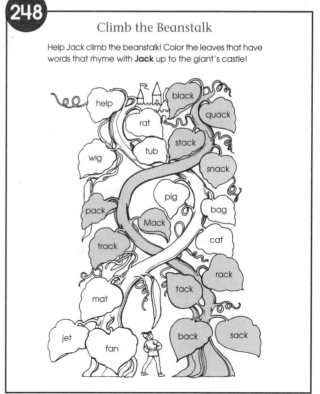

Leaves: help, black, quack, rat, stack, wig, tub, snack, pig, bag, pack, Mack, cat, track, rack, mat, tack, jet, fan, back, sack

249

Match the Opposites

The giant was big, and Jack was small. **Big** and **small** have **opposite** meanings. Read the words below. Draw lines to match the words with opposite meanings.

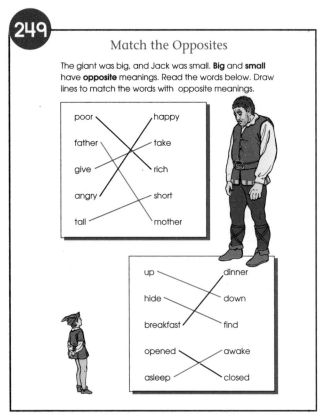

poor — rich
father — mother
give — take
angry — happy
tall — short

up — down
hide — find
breakfast — dinner
opened — closed
asleep — awake

250

What Is That?

Short a is the vowel sound you hear in **Jack**. Color the spaces with words that have the **short a** sound. What do you see?

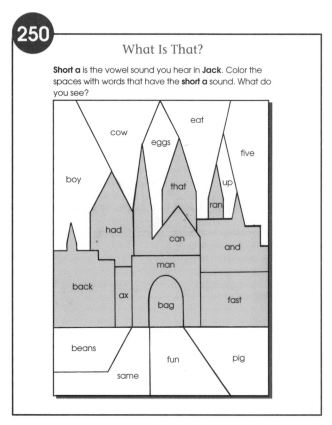

eat
cow
eggs
five
boy
that
up
had
ran
can
and
man
back
ax
bag
fast
beans
fun
pig
same

251

Order, Please

Read the words from the story. Underline the first letter of each word. Then, write them in ABC order.

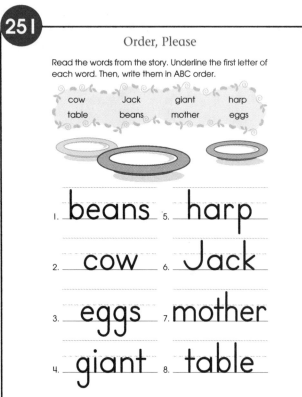

cow   Jack   giant   harp
table   beans   mother   eggs

1. beans   5. harp
2. cow   6. Jack
3. eggs   7. mother
4. giant   8. table

252

Scrambled Sentences

A **telling sentence** begins with a capital letter and ends with a period. Write the words in order to make telling sentences.

1. magic the were beans

The beans were magic.

2. beanstalk Jack the climbed

Jack climbed the beanstalk.

3. took he the harp

He took the harp.

4. woke giant the up

The giant woke up.

5. beanstalk cut the Jack

Jack cut the beanstalk.

253

Sort It Out

Cut out the pictures below and on page 255. Put them in the correct order to tell the story of "The Ugly Duckling."

1

2

3

4

255

Sort It Out (page 2)

5

6

7

8

9

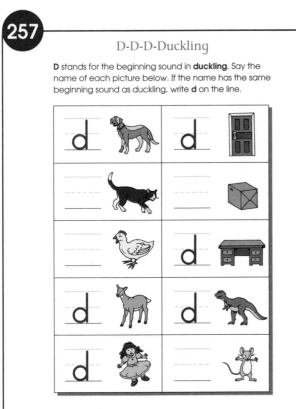

257

D-D-D-Duckling

D stands for the beginning sound in **duckling**. Say the name of each picture below. If the name has the same beginning sound as duckling, write **d** on the line.

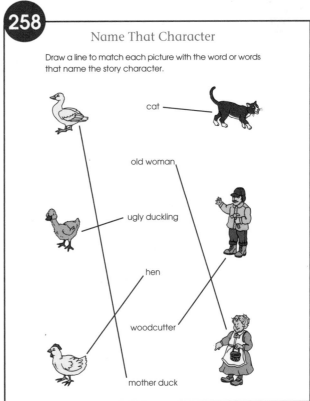

258

Name That Character

Draw a line to match each picture with the word or words that name the story character.

cat

old woman

ugly duckling

hen

woodcutter

mother duck

259

Tell Me Why

Match each sentence beginning with the correct ending. Write the letter of the ending on the line. The completed sentences will tell what happened and why it happened.

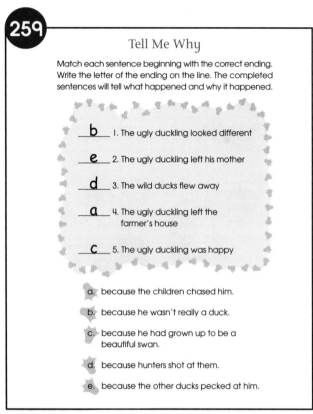

__b__ 1. The ugly duckling looked different

__e__ 2. The ugly duckling left his mother

__d__ 3. The wild ducks flew away

__a__ 4. The ugly duckling left the farmer's house

__c__ 5. The ugly duckling was happy

a. because the children chased him.

b. because he wasn't really a duck.

c. because he had grown up to be a beautiful swan.

d. because hunters shot at them.

e. because the other ducks pecked at him.

261

Say It Another Way (page 2)

"**He is** big and strong." He's

"**I am** so glad you are here." I'm

"The duckling **could not** lay eggs." couldn't

"Please **do not** be mean to me." don't

"**You are** a swan." You're

"Swans **are not** ugly." aren't

262

Action!

Verbs are words that show action. The words in the list are verbs. Write a verb from the list to complete each sentence.

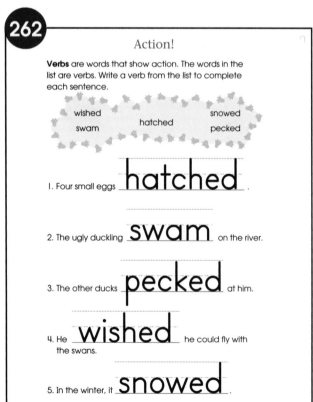

wished   snowed
swam   hatched   pecked

1. Four small eggs hatched

2. The ugly duckling swam on the river.

3. The other ducks pecked at him.

4. He wished he could fly with the swans.

5. In the winter, it snowed .

263

Opposites

The words **ugly** and **beautiful** have **opposite** meanings. Read the story words in the first column. Draw lines to match words with opposite meanings.

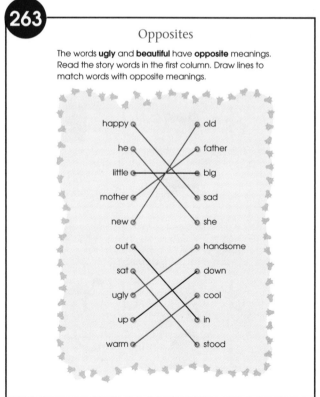

happy — sad
he — she
little — big
mother — father
new — old

out — in
sat — stood
ugly — handsome
up — down
warm — cool

264

"Hatch" the Eggs

The **short e** sound is the vowel sound in **nest**. Say the name of each picture. If the picture name has the same vowel sound as **nest**, color the picture to "hatch" the egg.

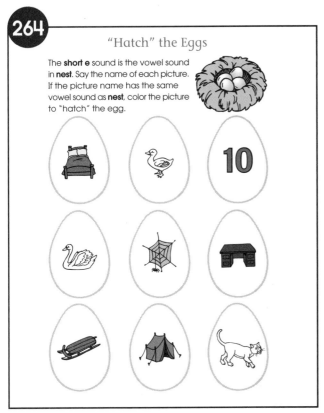

265

Who Said That?

Cut out the pictures of the characters. Glue the pictures beside the words the characters said.

267

Get It in Order

Cut out each set of pictures. Put them in the correct order. Retell each fable to a friend or family member.

269

Story Words

Write a word from the list to complete each sentence.
Hint: If you need help reading a word, find it in the story. Reread the sentence the word is in.

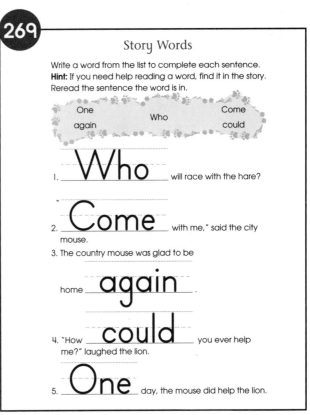

270

Write and Race

Put the words in alphabetical order to get the tortoise around the track. Work slowly and steadily. Don't wake up the hare!

cheer goose slow hare
wind day lesson fast

1. cheer
2. day
3. fast
4. goose
5. hare
6. lesson
7. slow
8. wind

271

Means the Same

Read the word that names the picture. Then, write a word from "The Hare and the Tortoise" that has almost the same meaning. If you need help, look back at the story.

hare — rabbit
tortoise — turtle
brag — boast
fast — quick
hopped — jumped
happy — glad

272

Vowel Sound Race

You can hear the **short a** sound in **brag**. You can hear the **long a** sound in **race**. Write the words from the list under the correct heading.

can day pass flag take
may ran fast late say

Short a Words

can
pass
flag
ran
fast

Long a Words

day
take
may
late
say

273

Finding Her Way Home

One		More Than One	
goose		geese	
bear		bears	

Help the country mouse find her way home. Trace the path with words that mean **more than one**.

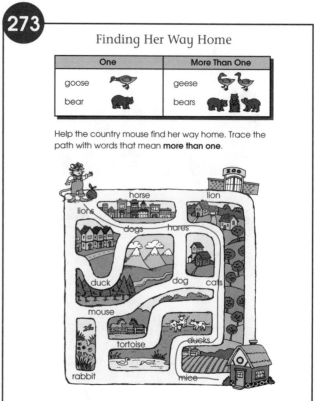

274

Alike and Different

Read the words. Draw a line to the mouse the words tells about. If the words tell about both mice, draw a line to both of them.

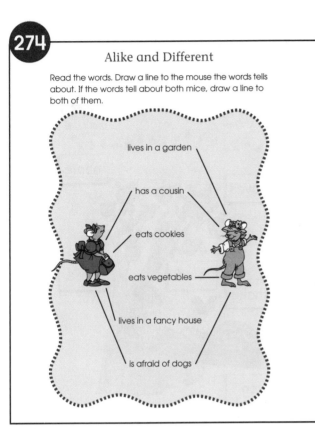

lives in a garden

has a cousin

eats cookies

eats vegetables

lives in a fancy house

is afraid of dogs

275

A Meal for a Mouse

Mouse and **meal** begin with the sound of **m**. Say the name of each picture. If the name begins with the **m** sound, write **m** to complete the word.

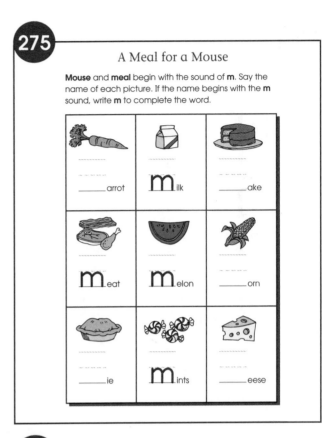

_____arrot   **m**ilk   _____ake

meat   **m**elon   _____orn

_____ie   **m**ints   _____eese

279

Story Sounds

Some words sound like what they mean. Write the word to tell the sound that is made in each picture.

Snap!   Meow!
Honk!   Screech!   Bang!

Screech!

Snap!

Bang!

Meow!

Honk!

280

Aesop's Lessons

Read each story lesson. Then, draw a line from the lesson to the character who learned the lesson.

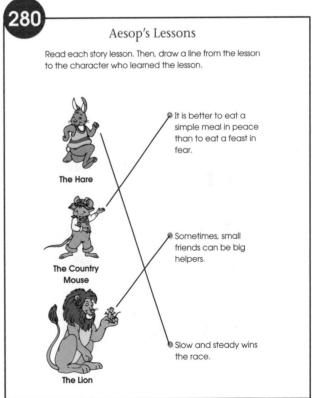

The Hare

The Country Mouse

The Lion

It is better to eat a simple meal in peace than to eat a feast in fear.

Sometimes, small friends can be big helpers.

Slow and steady wins the race.

281

Map Johnny's Life

Read the sentences about John Chapman's life. Number the sentences to show the order in which they happened. Draw a line on the map to show where Johnny traveled.

4 Johnny spent his last days in Indiana.

2 Johnny planted his first apple trees in Pennsylvania.

1 Johnny was born in Massachusetts.

3 Johnny planted many orchards in Ohio.

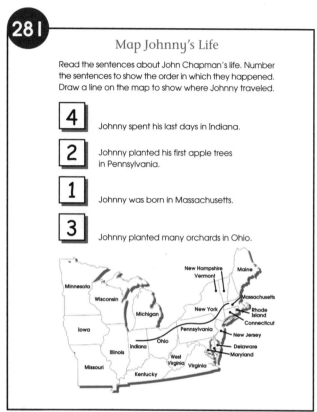

282

Words and Pictures

Write story words from the list to label the pictures.

leaves   tree   bird
apple   log   snake

285

Noun Sort (page 2)

Sort the nouns. Glue each picture from page 283 in the correct column.

People	Places	Things
settler	river	canoe
Native American	Indiana	fire
baby	school	log

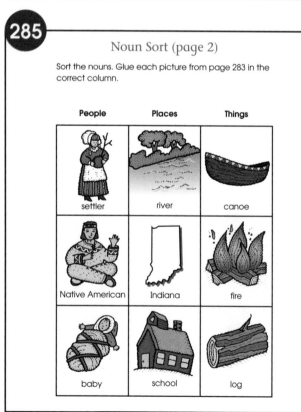

286

How Apple Trees Grow

Look at the pictures that show how apple trees grow. Draw a line from each picture to the sentence that tells about it.

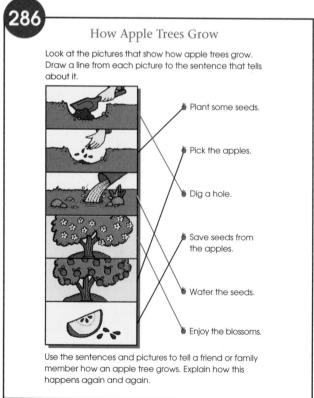

Plant some seeds.

Pick the apples.

Dig a hole.

Save seeds from the apples.

Water the seeds.

Enjoy the blossoms.

Use the sentences and pictures to tell a friend or family member how an apple tree grows. Explain how this happens again and again.

287
Find the Way

Help Johnny Appleseed reach the river. Trace the path with words that have the **long e** sound you hear in the word **seed**.

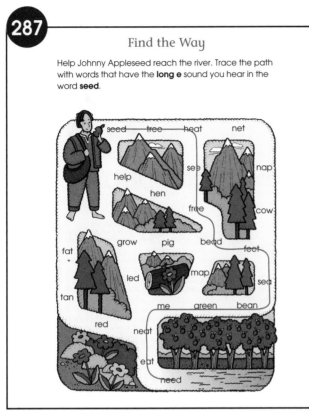

288
All About Johnny

Write a word from the story to complete each sentence. Write one letter on each line. Then, write the letters from the shaded boxes in order on the lines below to complete the last sentence. Look back in the story if you need to.

People said that Johnny . . .

wore a pot for a <u>h</u> <u>a</u> <u>t</u>.

loved to eat <u>a</u> <u>p</u> <u>p</u> <u>l</u> <u>e</u> <u>s</u>.

liked to help <u>p</u> <u>e</u> <u>o</u> <u>p</u> <u>l</u> <u>e</u>.

kept a pet <u>w</u> <u>o</u> <u>l</u> <u>f</u>.

planted apple <u>t</u> <u>r</u> <u>e</u> <u>e</u> <u>s</u>.

walked to <u>I</u> <u>n</u> <u>d</u> <u>i</u> <u>a</u> <u>n</u> <u>a</u>.

made a canoe from a <u>l</u> <u>o</u> <u>g</u>.

played with a family of <u>b</u> <u>e</u> <u>a</u> <u>r</u> <u>s</u>.

walked barefoot in the <u>s</u> <u>n</u> <u>o</u> <u>w</u>.

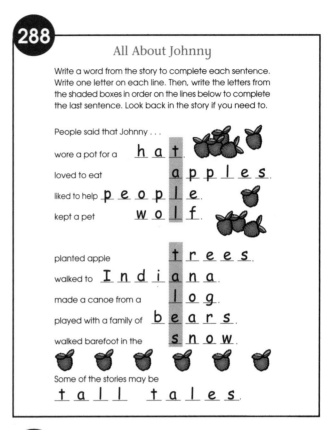

Some of the stories may be

<u>t</u> <u>a</u> <u>l</u> <u>l</u>   <u>t</u> <u>a</u> <u>l</u> <u>e</u> <u>s</u>.

289
A Pot for a Hat

People say Johnny wore a pot for a hat. **Pot** has the **short o** sound. Color the picture if its name has the **short o** sound.

290
The Ballad of Johnny Appleseed

Rhyming words have the same ending sound. **Seeds** and **weeds** are rhyming words. Finish each rhyme by writing the letters to complete the rhyming word.

When John Chapman was a boy,

Apples were his favorite t <u>o</u> <u>y</u>.

John left home as a young man.

He had some seeds and a good pl <u>a</u> <u>n</u>.

Johnny walked for miles and miles.

He left behind both trees and sm <u>i</u> <u>l</u> <u>e</u> <u>s</u>.

When you enjoy an apple tree,

Say, "Johnny planted this for m <u>e</u>."

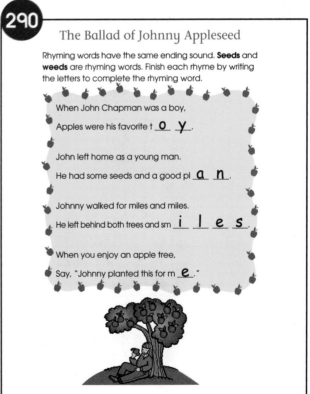

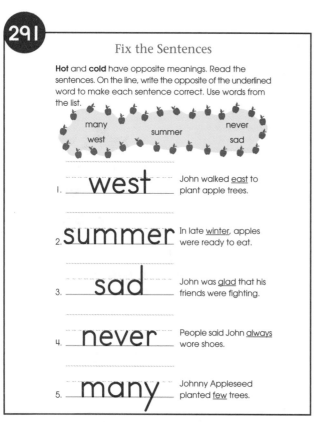

291

Fix the Sentences

Hot and **cold** have opposite meanings. Read the sentences. On the line, write the opposite of the underlined word to make each sentence correct. Use words from the list.

many   never

west   summer   sad

1. **west**   John walked <u>east</u> to plant apple trees.

2. **summer**   In late <u>winter</u>, apples were ready to eat.

3. **sad**   John was <u>glad</u> that his friends were fighting.

4. **never**   People said John <u>always</u> wore shoes.

5. **many**   Johnny Appleseed planted <u>few</u> trees.

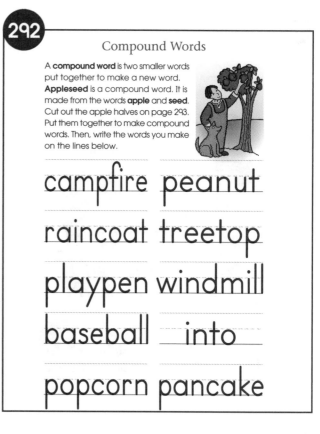

292

Compound Words

A **compound word** is two smaller words put together to make a new word. **Appleseed** is a compound word. It is made from the words **apple** and **seed**. Cut out the apple halves on page 293. Put them together to make compound words. Then, write the words you make on the lines below.

campfire   peanut

raincoat   treetop

playpen   windmill

baseball   into

popcorn   pancake

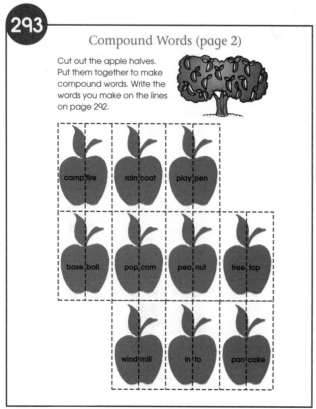

293

Compound Words (page 2)

Cut out the apple halves. Put them together to make compound words. Write the words you make on the lines on page 292.

camp fire   rain coat   play pen

base ball   pop corn   pea nut   tree top

wind mill   in to   pan cake

Everyday Learning Activities

Learning can become an everyday experience for your child. The activities on the following pages can act as a springboard for learning. Some of the suggested activities are structured and require readily available materials. Others may be used spontaneously as you are driving, shopping, or engaging in other everyday activities. The activities are arranged according to subject areas.

Reading

Previewing a Book Before reading a book aloud to your child, read the title and the author's name. Then, together, look at a few pictures (without giving away the ending) and have your child tell you what is happening in the illustrations on each page. Before you begin reading, encourage your child to tell what he or she thinks the story will be about.

Making Predictions As you read aloud together, encourage your child to predict what he or she thinks will happen next in the story. After you turn the page, look at the picture and check the prediction. Your child can then change or confirm the prediction. Making predictions should be fun, with a goal of making a logical guess as to what will happen next.

Matching Words Write key words from a favorite storybook on small cards. Have your child match each word to the word in the story. Then, read aloud the sentence where the word is found, and have your child read after you.

Listening for Context Clues One way to help your child recognize words when he or she is just beginning to read is to reread a familiar story, leaving out a key word (such as *giant* or *beanstalk)* in a sentence. Pause long enough for your child to supply the missing word.

Writing Dialogue After reading a favorite story together, have your child look at the pictures and tell what the characters are saying on each page. Write each suggestion on a stick-on note, and put it above the character's head. After you finish, reread the story aloud, but this time read only the dialogue on the stick-on notes.

Cooking Together You may wish to work with your child to prepare a recipe that relates to a book he or she has just read. For example, after reading about Johnny Appleseed, you might want to prepare homemade applesauce together and pretend you're pioneers as you enjoy it. Simple recipes are readily available in children's cookbooks. Some children's books even include story-related recipes, such as *Growing Vegetable Soup*, which has a vegetable soup recipe.

Word Riddles This game can be played in any room, in the car, or outside on a walk. Say riddles such as this one for your child to guess:

I see something wet. It starts with a **w**. What is it? *(water)*

I see something swimming. It starts with a **d**. What is it? *(duck)*

Once your child gets the hang of it, let him or her come up with riddles for you to guess. A variation is to ask riddles with rhyming words. For example:

I am up in the sky. I rhyme with spoon. *(moon)*

Word Wall As your child learns new words, begin a word wall by posting a large sheet of paper on his or her bedroom wall. Have your child write the new words on the paper. He or she may also draw a picture that illustrates the word. Encourage your child to add new words at least once a week.

Sock Puppets Use old socks, markers, and other materials such as scissors, glue, yarn, and felt to create sock puppets with your child. He or she may make puppets for story characters and act out the story. Your child may also create an unusual character and make up his or her own story with the puppet.

Word Bank Provide materials for your child to cover and decorate a small box to keep as a word bank. Your child can collect special words he or she wants to learn. As each word is collected, write it on a small card and slip it into the bank. Encourage your child to use words from the bank in his or her writing. At least once a week, remind your child to read the special words aloud.

Grocery Store Word Hunt Before going to the grocery store, give your child words such as the following that you have printed on index cards: *chocolate, orange, large, milk, green*. Have your child follow along as you shop, searching for the words from the cards.

Body Words Have your child lie down on a long sheet of white paper. Next, trace around his or her body. Let your child color in his or her clothes, eyes, face, and so on. Then, together, label the different parts of the body, such as *nose, chin, knee, arm,* and *neck*.

A New Ending After reading a favorite book, talk about how the story ends. Next, encourage your child to think up another ending. You may wish to have your child dictate the new ending as you write it down. Then he or she can illustrate it.

Mixed-Up Sentences On a heavy piece of paper, write a sentence from a story you have just read. Read the sentence with your child. Then, cut the words apart and mix them up. Have your child read the words and put them back in an order that makes sense. Examples:

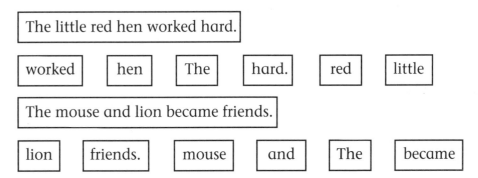

A Journal Buy your child a spiral-bound notebook to use as a journal for writing and drawing. Encourage him or her to write or draw in it every day. The journal should be private unless your child wants to share a picture or piece of writing.

Thank-You Notes It's never too early to say "Thank you!" After your child receives a gift, have him or her write or dictate a letter thanking the person who gave the present. Your child can also draw a picture in thanks. The sender of the gift will be thrilled with your child's good manners.

Pictures and Words Browse through a picture dictionary with your child. Point to different pictures, and have your child point to the word that goes with the picture. Read the definition aloud. If your child has started learning about alphabetical order, point out how the words are arranged.

Mathematics

Counting Encourage your child to count any small group of objects—carrots in a bag, pencils in a drawer, toys he or she is putting away. You might also separate objects into two different groups and have your child count both groups and add to see how many objects there are altogether.

Neighborhood Pets Have your child name all his or her friends' pets. Then, group the pets into categories, such as birds, cats, dogs, and gerbils. Together, make a bar graph to show how many pets there are of each kind. Your child can use the bar graph to tell which kinds of pets are the most popular.

Money Game Using play or real money, have your child count out one, two, three, four, and five pennies. Gather the pennies in a pile and have your child find groups of five pennies. Then, hold out a nickel and explain that it is worth five cents. Have your child make a group of pennies that is worth the same as the nickel. At another time, you may work with dimes and groups of ten pennies, two nickels, and so on. Work with your child from time to time until he or she can count out 99 cents.

Play Store Your child can put price tags (less than a dollar) on different items, such as plastic fruit, old toys, and other simple household items. Send your child to the "store" to buy a few different items. Then have him or her add up the prices. He or she can use real or play money to add up the amounts. You may also give your child play money and tell him or her to "buy" items within that amount. Work with your child to add up the purchases so as to stay within the budget.

Measure It! Encourage your child to make measurements of objects around the house. He or she can measure macaroni or rice with a measuring cup, his or her height (marked on a wall) with a ruler, the length of a pet, or water with measuring spoons and cups. While you are cooking, let your child measure out portions for recipes. Talk about the different units of measuring, such as for speed (miles per hour), distance (inches, feet, yards, miles), and volume (teaspoons, tablespoons, cups, pints, quarts, gallons). If you are comfortable with the metric system, you might want to mention those units as well.

Estimating Measurements After your child has some experience with measuring, let him or her estimate sizes and measure to check. For example, after measuring a few objects with a ruler, say "See if you can find five different things that are about ten inches long." After the items are gathered, help your child measure them to check. Point out that probably most of the things will not be exactly ten inches, but you are looking for objects that are close to ten inches. If your child's estimates are far off, wait a few days, meanwhile measuring other objects, and then let him or her try estimating again.

Driving Scavenger Hunt On a car trip, have your child go on a scavenger hunt. Make a list of things to spot, such as three cows, four red cars, ten cars with license tags that are from out of state, and so on. Your child can tally the items during the trip and see how long it takes to complete the list.

Finding Shapes Together with your child, cut out a triangle, a circle, a square, and a rectangle from construction paper. Then have your child choose one shape and find objects around the house that have the same shape. Repeat with the other shapes. **Hint:** Remind your child that it is only the shape he or she is looking for; objects may be any size and color, so long as the shape matches. You may also want to remind your child that any shape with three straight, connected sides is a triangle, and it need not be shaped exactly like the one you have cut out.

Social Studies

Mapping It Out Your child can make a map of the route to school. Walk together or take a ride along the route. Then work with your child to plot the turns and major twists along the roadway. He or she can help you place the major landmarks between your house and school, such as parks, stores, and other places of interest.

Where Does It Come From? When you get home from grocery shopping, have your child choose one food from the bag. Discuss how that food got from the farm or dairy to your house. Include how the food was grown or raised and by whom, how it got packaged and into a store, and then how it ended up in your own kitchen. You may find you'll need to do some research at the library or on the Internet.

Where in the World? State, country, and even world maps are important learning tools for first graders. Display different kinds of maps, helping your child explore the key and the different places shown. Locate where you live on the map and mark it with a pin, a highlighter, or stick-on note. When a particular place is mentioned in casual conversation or when a book your child is reading is set in a real place, refer to the map and help your child locate the place.

What People Do Your child can make a book about the people in your community who have different jobs. He or she can draw a picture of the person, name his or her job, and write a sentence about it. You may want to include your own picture, job title, and job description as a model. After the book is made, talk with your child about each career, and ask whether that would be a job your child would like and why or why not.

Science

The Food Pyramid Together with your child, draw on a large sheet of paper a food pyramid like the one shown. Discuss types of foods that go in each group (*Milk Group:* milk, yogurt, ice cream, cheese, pudding; *Meat Group:* fish, eggs, chicken, peanut butter, beef, peas and beans; *Vegetable Group:* tomatoes, spinach, broccoli, green beans, potatoes; *Fruit Group:* bananas, applesauce, strawberries, fruit juices; *Grain Group:* rice, bread, pasta, cereal, toast, crackers). Then, as you eat meals over a weekend, have your child draw a picture for each food he or she eats in its place on the grid. Discuss how well your child is eating, based on the daily requirements for a healthy diet.

Food Pyramid

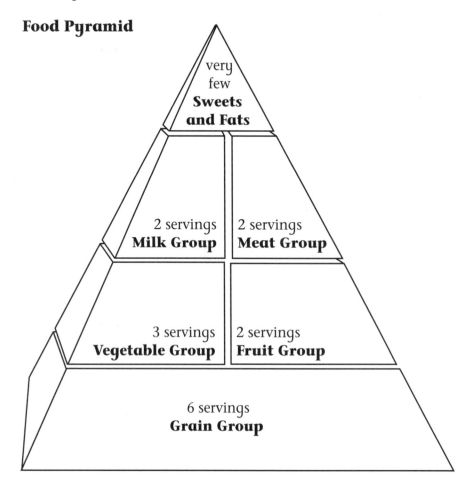

very few
Sweets and Fats

2 servings
Milk Group

2 servings
Meat Group

3 servings
Vegetable Group

2 servings
Fruit Group

6 servings
Grain Group

Nature Collection When your child is outside, collecting feathers or rocks can be a learning experience. Both can be found at the beach, in the park, or even in the backyard. Have your child compare and contrast the items he or she finds.

Bird Watching Hang a bird feeder outdoors in a place where you can see it from a window. As your child observes the birds, have him or her keep a log of what each type of bird looks like, when it comes to the feeder, and what kind of noises it makes. If you have a bird book, you can help your child identify the birds.

Fitness and Movement

Soccer Obstacle Course Make an obstacle course with outdoor objects. Then, have your child move a soccer ball with his or her feet along the course. Time your child, and then challenge him or her to beat the time by a few seconds.

Simon Says Play a simple game of "Simon Says" to help your child sharpen his or her auditory skills and physical coordination. Give directions such as the following: *Simon says do a jumping jack. Simon says touch your nose. Turn around.* Do each action as you give the suggestion, but remind your child to do what you say only if Simon says to do it.

Notes